To the Wonde nl

PSA

Ken D.
— 2015

Dancing with Baptists

a Vietnam era novel of racial divide and healing
forgiveness

Ken Bailey

Copyright © 2015 Ken Bailey

All rights reserved.

ISBN-10: 151729164X
ISBN-13: 978-1517291648

DEDICATION

To the Bride and the Groom in the hope of a second honeymoon soon.

Thou hast turned for me my mourning into dancing. Psalm 30:11 KJV

"She may cuss like any sailor,
She may party and romance.

She may read Balzac and Mailer,
Study law and high finance;

She may emulate Liz Taylor,
Purchase frocks in Paris, France,

But a girl while she's at Baylor
Better never ever dance."

-- John Thomas Baker,
Baylor University Class of 1940

CHAPTER 1

The Iron Triangle, South Vietnam

February 22, 1967

Chaplain (1ˢᵗ Lt.) Terrance L. "Chap" Bonner was Greg's second Black friend.

Chap held the bloody baby. Greg tied a clean shoestring around the baby's umbilical cord. He had an extra pair because the supply sergeant had gotten combat boot shoestrings in instead of the 3-0 silk sutures Greg had ordered.

Greg's experience cut the cord with the Metzenbaum scissors he wore on a chain next to his dog tags. After cutting the cord, Greg's attention switched back to the still squatting, still shivering fourteen-year-old in front of him. Greg dealt with the afterbirth. The mother of the moment finally laid back in the groundcover that surrounded them. She did not look at the baby in Chap's arms. The tiny infant's little fingers got tangled in the chain around Chap's neck. On the chain was a wooden cross that some of the village kids had carved as a gift for his birthday.

Now there was another birthday. Chap took the cross from around his neck with his left hand while he held the little guy in his right.

As the new mother lay on her post-opt bed of greenery, Greg bandaged the cut along her right temple. He marveled at how throughout the birth, like most Vietnamese mothers, she never made a sound. It was considered rude to make any noise in public.

Greg had not been on call that day. Chap had heard of a shrine he wanted to see and Greg wanted to be anywhere but the field operating tent. The last nineteen days had been pure hell. The people who made up the names called it *Operation Cedar Falls.* The intended objective was to drive Vietcong forces from the Iron Triangle, a sixty square mile area between the Saigon River and Route 13, a highway that stretched from Ho Chi Minh City to near the Cambodian border.

Nearly 16,000 American troops and 14,000 soldiers of the South Vietnamese Army had moved into the Iron Triangle. Seventy-two Americans were killed, many of them shot by snipers emerging from concealed tunnels. Seven hundred and twenty Vietcong were killed. It was easy for many to think, "Only seventy-two Americans," but five of those seventy-two had died on Greg's operating table.

Tens of tens had been saved but five boys died. Chap had prayed over the injured and the dead. Chap prayed while Greg and the surgeons reached deep into young abdomens invaded by bullets and shards of sharpened bamboo. After nineteen days of that, Greg and Chap needed the break.

The two walked and hitchhiked for hours and never found the shrine. It was Chap who had first spotted the young girl on the side of the road doubled over and bleeding from her forehead. Chap knelt and prayed for her. Greg helped her onto a wet patch of yellow Pintoi flowers that was partially hidden from the road. Moving the injured and pregnant girl off the dangerous shoulder happened just in time. A sputtering convoy kicked up shells, rocks, and dust and left tracks over the hula-hoop sized wet ground where the young mother's water had broken.

Chap took off his shirt and laid it on the ground next to the new mother. He bent over and placed the tiny one on it. The mother looked away. Many Vietnamese believed that if you show attention to a baby it alerts evil spirits and they will come to kill the baby.

Greg was the first to hear the next trucks. He and Chap ducked in the grass alongside the young Asian Madonna and child. As soon as the last olive-dipped-in-mud truck roared by, the barrel of an assault rifle nudged through the leaves of a dark green bush. Next an RPK machine gun pushed through a neighboring bush. One was pointed at Greg and the other at Chap's chest where the cross had been moments earlier. The Chaplain and the young surgical tech froze as a missed-matched uniformed teenager and a head-bandaged preteen followed their weapons out of the bushes.

The teenager expertly swung his shoulder-
strapped weapon around to his back and picked up the
fatigue-wrapped newborn. Chap's cross dangled from
the pocket of the jacket. Standing guard, the preteen's
dark eyes revealed his internal vote to kill the roadside
delivery team. Greg and Chap slowly backed away from
the bloody four. Chap raised his right hand and prayed.
"Lord Jesus, we pray for these young souls."

As Greg and Chap continued to back away,
the teenager helped the young mother to her feet and
within seconds they were gone. The only sign of new
life and possible death was the placenta on the
aluminum plants.

Three clicks down the road, both men paused
and took a moment. The shirtless Chaplain and the
bloody surgical tech spent the rest of the way back in
collective silence.

CHAPTER 2

The Near Northside, Houston, Texas

November 1951

Greg was not born a Baptist. He married into the Faith at age four. That was the year his mother wed Jack the Baptist. Greg's mother and Jack Baker were both divorced. Divorce was an ugly business in post-World War II Houston, but an almost unheard of circumstance at small Trinity Street Baptist Church.

Jack and Greg's mother were married at Jack's house. The nice enough, two bedroom, red brick home was on a tree-lined suburban street. Up until the wedding, Greg was Gregory W. Henderson, Jr., man of the house.

Greg never knew Gregory W. Henderson, Sr. "The Yankee" as Greg's maternal grandmother called his biological father, blew into Houston after the War, married, helped conceive Greg, and was gone before some guy in a white mask slapped Greg on the butt hard enough to make him cry. That was the last time anyone made Greg cry.

Trinity Street Baptist Church

1955

Greg seldom spoke in Sunday school, but he did pray. *Lord, please don't let her call on me to pray. Please Lord, you know I don't know how.* While he was afraid to pray out loud, for fear of being thought unholy or stupid, Greg was not afraid to speak up. Greg's sixty-nine-year-old Sunday school department leader, Mrs. DeHartman, had asked the department to learn to name all the books of the Bible. The first child to say all the names in the correct order would win a prize.

The first Sunday no one volunteered. Greg saw this as an opportunity to raise his status with the grownups and his peers. He went home that Sunday determined to memorize every book in order. He would be the first kid to list all the books.

Greg thought, *If Mrs. DeHartman was giving a prize, maybe it would be a Roy Rogers lunch box with a Trigger thermos.* But it was more likely to be something churchy, like a little tin coin bank with a picture of Jesus on it for the weekly offering.

Sunday came and Greg's confidence was high. He had worked hard all week. He had even skipped an episode of *Sergeant Preston of the Yukon* to study.

In Sunday School, Greg usually sat in the back with the other boys until someone had to separate them. That morning Greg fearlessly sat in the third row. He positioned himself in the space between Melinda and Shauna who were sitting in front of him. He had the perfect view of Mrs. DeHartman and she could see him clearly when his volunteering hand shot up. Greg had practiced raising his hand with lightning speed, like Wyatt Earp drawing his Colt Buntline Special.

As Melinda and Shauna leaned in and out to whisper to each other, Greg would bob his head like Rocky Marciano to maintain eye contact with Mrs. DeHartman. He didn't even open his hymnal in order to keep his raising-hand free.

Sunday school time always moved slower than kickball time or *Sky King* time. That Sunday's assembly moved so slowly it was like Friday waiting-for-the-three o'clock-bell-time. Then suddenly he heard,

"Who is prepared to recite the books of the Bible?"

In his excitement to raise his hand, Greg's Baptist Hymnal fell off his lap and onto the floor with a thud. An embarrassing gale of laughter erupted and while Greg bent to retrieve his song book he heard the worst sound he had ever heard in his young life,

"Ruth? Is that your hand up?"

"Yeth, Ma'am," Ruth said.

Mrs. Dehartman was delighted. Ruth Morrison was an Orphan Annie-haired brain with eyeglasses. She stood there before the entire class with the confidence of a bull fighter and the lisp of a three-year-old.

"Methyou, Mark, Luke, John,"

All right, Greg thought, *She doesn't know the Old Testament.*

"Wait. Thaw-wee," Ruth corrected. "Genethith, Exoduth…"

Greg was devastated.

"Wonderful. Wasn't that wonderful class?" Mrs. DeHartman said as she encouraged the children to applaud. Then she walked over to the upright piano, stepped behind it and pulled out a brown sack with something in it too big to be a tin offering box.

"I don't know why, but I thought a boy would be the first to say the books," Mrs. DeHartman apologized, "but you can return it for a Dale Evans one."

Ruth's smile broadened so wide the corners of her mouth almost reached her Spoolied curls.

"Oh, thank you, Mithus DeThartman. I just love Roy Rogerths and Twigger!"

Greg never did get up and say the books of the Bible. Ruth Morrison later married one of the guys who invented the Hacky Sack. Greg always figured she wooed him with his rightfully due Roy Rogers lunch box with the "Twigger" thermos.

Because of his earlier divorce, Jack the Baptist

could not be a deacon. At Trinity Street Baptist the
deacons ran   everything. If a preacher's belief about
anything ever differed from that of the deacons, the
preacher's parsonage had new inhabitants before one
could say the twenty-third psalm.

Greg was often friends with the preacher's kids
while they were there. Greg liked them because,
somehow, the fact that they had to be good made them
the most mischievous. The older P.K. boys usually
took one of two paths: going into the ministry like their
father, or going wild.

Soon after Greg and his mother married Jack
the Baptist, Greg went to his first funeral. It was for the
preacher's oldest son. The story was the seventeen-
year-old had been racing on a motorcycle, lost control,
went air borne, and was gruesomely skewered on a stop
sign. There was even talk of alcohol being involved.

Of course, Greg never heard any of that. He
just sat there in the Sunday pew on Saturday wondering
why everyone looked so sad. Before the actual service
started, Mrs. Renfrow took Greg and the other children
outside to play.

Until he was eight, Greg had to sit on that
Sunday pew with his mother every week. Then, for
some unknown reason, when he turned eight he was
sent to be with Jack and his friends after Sunday
school. They were all in their mid-to-late thirties and
non-deacons like Jack. At first Greg thought this might
be some kind of punishment. He had been pretty good,
for Greg, and hadn't gotten into any kind of trouble

with Raymond, the current P.K., for some time.

Greg's first Sunday with "The Men" was eye-opening. Greg finished Sunday school and instead of going on into Big Church, he walked down the hall to the locked door where the men collected. The room was kept locked because behind that door was the entire morning's take from the offering envelopes. Some Sundays the giving was as much as two hundred dollars and one can't be too careful about tempting Southern Baptist widow ladies with hard cash and shiny dimes.

Stoney let Greg in and locked the door behind him. Stoney was the tallest of the men. He always wore a big wide smile and an out-of-date tie. Greg did not know what any of the men did between Sundays, but he guessed Stoney was either a salesman or a pin spotter. Jack's was the next face he saw. Jack the Baptist was a good dresser and after he married Greg's mother, she saw to it that Greg also dressed well. That morning Greg was wearing a gray suit and tie from Battlestein's that made him look like a tiny mob boss.

Jack's shoes were always shiny. He taught Greg to shine his own shoes. Greg liked the smell of the polish. Jack kept all their supplies in a homemade wooden shine box under the kitchen sink. Greg liked the responsibility. Every Sunday morning he would place his right shoe on top of the heel rest on the lacquered wood handle. Then he would reach into the box and grab in order: old underwear with black Shinola splotches, a toothbrush to get polish into the stitched crease between the edge of the shoe and the sole, and either a shine cloth or brush. Jack had showed Greg how to roll the shine cloth like the Bible scrolls Greg made in Vacation Bible School. Greg would then pass the scrolled cloth behind his shoe and saw back and forth until the back of each shoe was shiny. Then he would do the toes. Sometimes, when no one was around, Greg would spit on the shoes. He was never sure why anyone would do that but he had seen it done on television.

Next to Jack and his shiny shoes sat Martin. Martin in his dark rimmed glasses looked like a doctor or a businessman to Greg. Martin sat in front of the dollar bills he was counting. The last of the men was Jelly. Jelly was the fattest man Greg had ever seen up close. Greg liked Jelly a lot. He was always cracking jokes, doing voices, and kidding around. Greg wondered if he had been a P.K. when he was little.

Jack counted the coins, Stoney transferred the "read my Bible" and other check-marked information on the envelopes into a large book. Jelly told stories about ball games and acted out Milton Berle bits from the Tuesday night television show. While the rest of the church sang *His Eye is on the Sparrow*, Greg's eyes filled with tears from laughing at Jelly's stories. Greg wasn't there five minutes when he knew this wasn't punishment.

But not all of Jelly's jokes got big laughs. Like the one about the people in a lifeboat after a ship sank.

"It was apparent to everyone," Jelly said, "that there were too many people in the lifeboat and they were taking on water. So a Frenchman got up, saluted, and said, 'Viva la France!' and jumped overboard. Next an Englishman got up, put his hand over his heart and said, 'Long Live the Queen!' and he jumped overboard. And then a Texan got up and said, 'Remember the Alamo!' and he threw a Meskin' overboard." Jelly, Stoney, and Martin laughed so loud Greg was afraid they could be heard down the hallway and into the sanctuary. Greg laughed but didn't get it. Jack smiled but didn't laugh.

Trinity Street Baptist Church

Another Sunday 1955

After the folding money and coins were counted, they were placed in a zippered brown bank bag. Now it was time for the fun to begin. Between Sunday School and church, Jack, the other men, and Greg would escort the approximately one hundred and seventy dollars to the bank. Being Sunday, the bank, of course, was closed. Texas blue laws also kept grocery stores, department stores, cleaners, and just about every other business in town closed.

Jack would drive. Martin rode shotgun without a shotgun or any other weaponry as far as Greg knew. Greg had to ride the hump in the middle of the back seat. He was squeezed in between large Stoney and extra-large Jelly. Jack would drive to nearby North Main Bank and up to the night depository. Within seconds, the bank bag disappeared and they were off.

Why it took four grown men and a kid to stuff one bag into the night depository was a troubling question for Greg. A question Greg never asked.

Had he asked, Greg might have been excommunicated from the best part of church, Wally's Restaurant. Wally's was a 24-hour restaurant halfway back to the church. The four men plus Greg would stop each week for four coffees and a chocolate milk. Greg never had chocolate milk at home.

Even though they never prayed over their coffee or talked about Jesus at Wally's, Greg sensed a warm closeness between these men. They didn't share Jesus with the waitress but they did kid with her and leave a nice tip. Greg got a sense that the entire restaurant was happy to see them during their short visit every Sunday. A quiet eight-year-old can learn a lot about life and being a man between bank and church over coffee and chocolate milk.

By the time Greg and the men returned to the church, the singing would be over and the preaching begun. Instead of going into church late, Greg would sit alone in the Fellowship Hall. He could hear the preaching over a loud speaker in case his Mother asked him any questions about the message. At the same time, he could play with the plastic cowboys he had hidden in his pockets.

One Sunday when Greg walked into Fellowship
Hall, Emmett, the Janitor's son, was sitting on the floor
playing jacks. Emmett stared at Greg for a minute, not
sure what to do. Both boys knew not to talk out loud.
Greg sat at his regular seat under the overhead speaker.
Emmett went back to his jacks. After a couple of
minutes Greg eased a plastic cowboy out of his dress
pants. He reached back in his pocket and brought out
two more. Emmett was now watching Greg and his
growing array of good guys and bad guys. Greg was
uncomfortable being stared at. He started to reposition
his chair when Emmett got up off the floor and walked
over. Now it was Greg's turn to watch.

Emmett placed a jack on the table to steady one
of Greg's cowboys that was no longer able to stand
because Greg chewed off the base. Emmett put down
two more jacks behind two more cowboys. Greg was
not sure what Emmett had in mind until… bam!
Emmett rolled his red jacks ball into the cowboys and
knocked two on the ground. Greg jumped. Emmett
jumped when Greg jumped. Greg looked at his downed
cowboys and the red ball still rolling across the room.

Laughter shot out of his mouth like Emmett's
ball. There was never laughing allowed. Greg was never
in time for the pre-sermon joke and almost never got
them anyway. But this was funny. Both hands covering
his mouth could not keep the sound of laughter from
spilling around his fingers. Emmett smiled big and
retrieved his ball and the floored cowboys. Now it was
Greg's turn as Emmett handed him the ball.

Greg didn't know it, but Emmett's church had

been bombed and they could not meet there until the church was repaired. For almost two months the boys would meet in Fellowship Hall and play, and sometimes listen to the preacher. Emmett was Greg's first Black friend.

Greg never thought much about who was Black or White or Mexican back then. But sometimes it just jumped up and surprised him. Like the time Wally put up the new sign. *We reserve the right to refuse service to anyone.* Greg asked what the sign meant. Greg never asked questions. The men stalled and then Jelly said laughingly, "No, jungle bunnies." Only Jelly laughed this time. Greg was starting to question just how funny Jelly was.

When Greg was a couple of years younger, one of his mother's favorite stores was Sears Roebuck on North Shepherd. While his mother tried on dresses, Greg was allowed to roam, "just not too far."

Over by the Boy Scout display of uniforms and sashes were two water fountains. Each of the white porcelain structures rose out of the floor tile and blossomed to a bowl with a small chrome fountain. A small ship's wheel-like chrome knob on the side turned to release the cool water. Above the twin fountains were signs. The one on the right said, "Whites Only," the other "Colored Only."

Greg stood there wondering what would

happen if he drank from the wrong one. Then he thought, *I guess this is why Mrs. Smith taught us to read.*

Sometimes, on really hot summer Sundays, the boys would sneak into the church kitchen to see if anyone had left a Coca Cola in the refrigerator. While Greg shared that cold Coke with Emmett he never once thought of those water fountains at Sears.

Small Trinity Street Baptist was probably the birthplace of "Don't ask, don't tell." No one there drank, cussed, fooled around on their wives, or was gay. Gerrod Blackstone, the music minister, was a "confirmed bachelor" at 34. Marcie Williams and LuAnn Sutton lived in that one bedroom garage apartment because it was cheaper. The one thing that was out in the open, and often inside, was smoking.

Four of the seven deacons smoked. The church provided a smoking area out back for those who struggled to sit through an entire sermon. Greg saw a few non-smokers out there on occasion, as well.

But now smoking was becoming a Baptist issue and Greg heard earfuls about it.

The Baptists had actually taken on the tobacco issue much earlier. At the 1937 Southern Baptist Convention an amendment to a social resolution stated:

It is the sense of this Convention that the prevalence of smoking among Christian people, especially among preachers, church leaders, and denominational workers, is not only detrimental to the health of those who participate, but is hurtful to the cause of Christ in that it weakens the message and lowers the influence of those who are charged with the preservation and spread of the Gospel. Washington D.C. 1937

But during World War II cigarettes were given out for free and the *Smoke 'em if you've got 'em'* break was often one of the few breaks available. Consequently, the soldiers who returned home from World War II had taken up the habit and nobody was going to tell them what to do. That attitude was seen throughout Baptist life. Trinity Street, like all other Baptist churches, was autonomous, the epitome of an independent church and people to whom no one, this side of Heaven and the Word of God, was going to tell what to do.

These deacons had fought and laid in blood and mud next to the bodies of their dead buddies, praying they would not be next. "I carried a gun and fired it so that no Nazi or Jap or anyone else was going to have me saluting their flag and spewing out their evil doctrine," one of the smoking deacons coughed.

"They've quit preachin' and gone to meddlin'," complained another deacon.

Jack the Baptist had never smoked. He also had never served in World War II. He had tried to enlist but an inner ear problem that did not show up until his enlistment physical kept him from it. Being a divorced, non-veteran in a small church like Trinity Street Baptist embarrassed Jack. Greg never heard him speak about the war or the divorce. He did talk to Greg about smoking. Jack the Baptist had lettered in track in high school. He had attributed part of his speed and lung power to not smoking. This impressed young Greg more than any school lecture or Public Service Announcement.

CHAPTER 3

Camp Dong Tam, Mekong Delta,

South Vietnam

February 23, 1967

Greg and shirtless, cross-less Chap got back to Dong Tam just in time for 4 a.m. breakfast mess. Chap and Greg each went to their quarters, got cleaned up, and met back at 0415 hours.

Camp Dong Tam was brand new. Only months earlier the area was inundated with Mekong rice paddies. Now the silt and sand pumped off the bottom of the Song River over-filled enough rice patties to create a 600 acre muddy camp. General Westmoreland, commander of all U.S. military operations, said Dong Tam was a place where you could be up to your knees in mud and have sand blow in your eyes. But he had placed Dong Tam there with a purpose. First, it was to be headquarters for the almost 20,000 troops of the 9th Infantry Division. Second, it was to make a clear statement.

The Mekong Delta of South Vietnam was the operational base for a large division of Viet Cong *Việt Nam Cộng-sản* (a contraction for Vietnamese Communists). Westmoreland chose the location as a strong message to say to the communists, "We are here in the Mekong and we are here to stay."

————————

Greg arrived starving at the mess hall. It appeared he had beaten Chap there. The Buckinghams' hit "Kind of a Drag" was playing on "Dawn Buster", an Armed Forces Radio Network program. The show still opened with "Goooooooooooooood Morning Vietnam!" even though the Air Force Sergeant who coined the opening, Adrian Cronauer, had ended his tour of duty months earlier.

Greg grabbed a tray and started down the line. Even at breakfast, a Himalayan-sized pile of rice was on line for all the local troops that would eat there. Greg pushed his tray to the eggs, bacon, hash browns, milk, and more section. With a loaded tray he started to navigate the tables filled with too-tired, too-sleepy, too-homesick soldiers who had no interest in unknown company.

Then Greg spotted Chap stepping into the line. Greg stood and waited and soon the two crossed to the empty end of a just policed folding table. They had only been seated for a minute when Chap said to Sgt. Franklin, "Come sit with us."

Oh great, Greg thought.

Greg had gotten to Dong Tam only a few days before Franklin arrived. They were both the same rank. Franklin was a good surgical tech. He was a "never" guy. Never missed, never late, never joked, never smiled. However, one "never" Greg would have appreciated was "never talked". But that was not the case. Franklin talked and talked a lot. It was always the same; the plight, abuse, and secret conspiracy of genocide of the Black man. In fact, Franklin was not Franklin at all. He demanded to be called by his African name. Greg could never remember how to pronounce his African name. This was not helped by the fact his fatigues and duty uniforms were all labeled Franklin. Chap, Greg, and Franklin were three of only a small number at the camp who didn't carry a weapon. Greg thought that was probably a good idea.

When Greg was in medic school at Shepherd AFB, they told him he would be issued a sidearm if he went into any "hot" areas. However, because of the Geneva Convention, he could only fire on the enemy if they were trying to kill his patient. Greg would not be allowed to return fire if they were trying to kill him. Medics were not supposed to be targeted by the enemy. Greg asked his instructor incredulously, "So I'm there in the jungle. I'm treating a patient and I have to decide whether Charlie is aiming at <u>me</u> or the wounded guy I'm sewing up before I return fire?" The instructor continued without answering.

"So, how's it going, Bro?" Chap asked Franklin. Greg was thinking Chap probably didn't know how to say Franklin's African name either.

"Aw, you know, S.O.S." Franklin cleaned up his language out of respect for the Chaplain. But Chap had heard it all and simply ignored it unless someone took the Lord's name in vain. Chap heard more profanity everyday than Vietnamese and he heard a lot of Vietnamese. One Sunday a quarter he would work a little Book of James "controlling the tongue" into a sermon, but like the Marines there, Chap picked his fights carefully and well.

One of his greatest challenges was when someone thought it was funny to hide his portable pulpit. Chap would sling an old rucksack containing the traveling wooden pieces on his back and go into the most dangerous areas in the Delta. Within seconds of getting to any group of troops, he could "shuck his ruck" and assemble those pieces of wood into a holy reminder of heavenly places. He held services for Catholics and Protestant G.I.'s and, when there was no rabbi in the bush, he would observe rice paddy Shabbat services.

But when his traveling pulpit would come up hidden again, it was all Chap could do to not grab a gun and say, "For the 40th time where's my fugazzi ruck?"

"Greg and I are going to pray for our breakfasts. How can we pray for you?" Chap asked the sergeant.

"Forget me, pray for the brothers in Detroit."

"What about the brothers?" Chap asked sincerely.

Franklin looked at Greg, then around, then back at Chap, "I ain't saying nothing but there's gonna' be a long hot summer."

"Why's that?" Greg asked.

Franklin stared at Greg. Franklin sees a cracker from Texas asking questions about things about which he has no clue. But Franklin did respect Greg as a fellow tech. And the fact that Greg hung out with a Black guy was points in his favor; but he was still a cracker from Texas.

Greg saw Franklin as a privileged, educated Black man who was pretending to be one of the oppressed so he could bitch about all the cards being stacked against him and use it for an excuse were he ever to fail. Just as Chap stayed prayed ahead, Franklin stayed pissed ahead.

Chap saw both men as children of God struggling to survive life in a world that wanted them both dead.

"Why don't you give Greg a little insight into what's going on back home from your point of view?" Chap moderated.

"Like he gives a-," Franklin said.

Greg grabbed the edge of his tray and started to rise and move to another table.

"Wait," Franklin said. "I know the docs and nurses and the white techs think I'm a Black Panther or something."

"I never heard anybody say that," Greg replied.

"You just think I'm a stupid field hand wanting to break into Master's house for some Virginia ham and corn pone, don't you?" Franklin asked.

"No, I see you more as a fried trout and hush puppies kind of guy."

"This ain't funny white boy. People are dying back home."

"People are dying here too. All colors."

"But here, we are armed by the government. If we fight back we are not thrown in jail or given the electric chair."

"What do you want from me?" Greg asked sincerely.

"I don't want anything from you. I just want to serve my time, get out of here in one piece and get back home to help."

"I think that's something we can all agree on," teamed Chap.

"How 'bout I pray for our food?" Chap offers. "Father God, father to us all, we pray for the oppressed and wronged people everywhere. We pray for safety and if it is your will that we do get back home to help. And Lord God, I pray for by brother Abidemi,"

That was it, Abidemi, Greg thought. *Chap did know it.*

"Give him peace and discernment to take on causes anointed by you and to love where he can. But if he is called to be a deliverer like Ehud of old, I pray that his fight is your fight and that injustices are righted by your mighty hand. And I pray for my brother Greg. Thank you for his friendship and struggle to understand all that he is being exposed to here and for his Melinda back home that they can be reunited to serve and love together under you. Oh, and for whatever this is we are eating. In Jesus name. Amen." Chap finished.

Greg, Chap and Abidemi each took a bite of breakfast.

"Tell me again why you chose Abidemi? And what it means?" Greg asked.

"What does Greg mean?" Franklin/Abidemi asked back.

"It means I was named after a guy who stayed around long enough to make me and left me nothing but his name," Greg said. Greg's answer took Franklin back a bit.

"Mine means pretty much the same thing," Franklin said. "Abidemi means 'born during a father's absence.'"

"You two could be brothers," Chap smiled. The three continued eating. Chap was about to tell Abidemi about their adventure with the young mother when Greg decided to keep the conversation going.

"You ever meet Martin Luther King?"

"You think cause I'm Black we all know each other? You know Johnny Unitas? Stupid cracker."

"Virginia ham-eatin' - ," Greg countered.

Right on time, J.L. sauntered up. "Hey Doc, you still leaving 'em in stitches? How's it hangin'? Thumper. Abidemi"

Technical Sergeant Jefferson Lincoln Jackson the third, J.L. to everyone on base, had a nickname for everyone. He called Greg "Stitch" or sometimes, like many of the other medics, "Doc". He called Chap, Thumper, short for Bible Thumper, and Abidemi was enough for Franklin.

Sgt. J.L. was dark-skinned, with white-gray hair and matching bushy eyebrows. His too large belly put tension on his medic uniform shirt exposing gray belly hair between strained buttons that could rocket launch with one big belch. He had an old school confidence, and gout from too much high living in low-down places that gave him a limp and an occasional wince when he made an awkward step. He was crude, rude, and tattooed and everybody loved him. He was welcomed at any table from the top brass to the scared, fresh off the boat airman. So, when he joined Greg, Chap, and Franklin, the toned turned J.L.'s way. J.L. led with one of his off-color jokes that made Chap uncomfortable; but like Jelly back home, J.L. got a larger portion of forgiveness that matched his size.

"What is it, my brother? J.L. said to Franklin, "Look like you stressin' more than a gook caught in tanglefoot."

Greg envied the way the old Sarge used words like *tanglefoot*. He painted pictures with words that usually had a punch line. Like this image of Charlie caught in ankle-high barbed wire. Soldiers would weave the cutting wire into a spiked mesh and surround their location with it. Anyone trying to sneak up on them would be slowed and hopefully stopped long enough to be captured or killed.

"Just trying to teach White Bread here a little about the struggle," Franklin told J.L.

"Man, you need to let that go for a bit. I mean loosen the bone Wilma! That stuff's gonna' make you crazy. Stitch here is okay."

"Now don't sit there all U.N. on me and act like you aren't bothered by the way we are treated." Franklin was becoming agitated again.

"Sure, it bothers me. But even Groucho takes the cigar out of his mouth sometime."

"Tell Casper here about you in Korea."

"You served in Korea?" Greg asked.

"Oh man, it's five in the morning. Why I have to go over all that now?"

Abidemi glared at J.L.

"All right. Yeah, I was drafted into the infantry back then."

"Army?" Greg asked.

"U.S. Army?" Chap added trying to lighten things.

"Air Force came later." J.L. explained.

"Tell him," Franklin demanded.

"The part Cassius Clay here,"

"Muhammed Ali," Franklin corrected.

"Wants me to tell- Have you heard this Padre?"

Chap shook his head "Don't think so."

"So, I was just a kid, barely nineteen, dumped in South Korea with no anger toward anyone on that whole island; North, South, East or West. But I did have a want. I wanted to be a part of the 24th. You know about the 24th?"

Greg shook his head.

"He don't know nothin'," Franklin added.

"Do you want me to tell this or not? And watch your mouth," the older Black man ordered the younger.

Then he turned back to Greg, "This is the story you don't get in your oatmeal-box-looking, founding-honky-fathers history classes. This was how it really was." J. L. said.

Franklin smiled for the first time in Greg's memory.

"Let's keep the story going," Chap cajoled.

"Well, back in the day, we're talking early 1850's, colored soldiers were put off to themselves. Everybody thought we were too stupid to shoot or duck and might get some Yankee boy's fancy uniform all messy with blood.

After the Civil War before 1870, I think, the 24th Infantry Regiment was born. A lot of the soldiers were either veterans from Colored infantry Regiments or freemen. Have you heard of the Buffalo Soldiers?"

Greg wasn't sure but he shook his head "yes" to not interrupt the story."

"Well they were part of the 24th."

"Really?" a surprised Chap responded but the storyteller did not miss a beat.

"In every war they distinguished themselves. So, here I am in 1951 Korea and there's a chance I could be part of this group. So, I put in my request and they look at me like I'm crazy.

'Boy, don't you know nothing?' This pasty white, pencil-necked corporal asked me. Before I can react to his customary rudeness with an instant dental extraction he pushes a base paper my way.

'You <u>can</u> read, can't you?' he smartassed my way." Chap and Greg are silent while J. L. relives the tension of that time. J.L. makes a tight fist without realizing it. Then as his fist unclenched, "During my time in the stockade for punching that little weasel-" J. L.'s two-pack-a-day cough mixed with a big laugh paused the story.

"I got the true scuttlebutt from other inmates who knew the whole truth about the 24th."

Suddenly some story in the back of Greg's mind came forward. *24ᵗʰ Colored Division.*

"Wait, was this the colored -, I mean Black soldiers that caused the riot in Houston?"

"No. They didn't 'cause' nothin'. They were 'caused' upon." J. L.'s laugh was gone.

Chap said, "Go on J.L."

The old Sarge got back on track and within moments had re-raised his momentum and was back to full speed ahead.

"Anyways, in WW II the 24th was back at it again. Killin' Japs and pissin' off white guys. No matter what hellhole they stationed them in, they succeeded. Then after the war in 1948 here comes Harry Truman. The President signs this order that there won't be any more segregation in the Armed Forces. Whew! More pissed off white guys. Truman cans the Secretary of the Army for refusing to let his little white boys play with the Negros."

"Okay," Afro-American Jelly was really getting fired up. "Here comes Korea. Even with all the segregation the 24th manages to mainly stay Black. Strapping on their bayonets they're pushing the Chinks all over the place. But then they get set-up."

"Set-up?" Greg asked and then got immediately quiet again.

"That's right. Set-up. They get pinned down. The enemy is all around them like Custer with a million little Charlie Chan's instead of Indians. They call in support and the next thing you know the story gets out that the colored soldiers dropped their weapons and started running around like hundreds of Stepin Fetchits."

"Dirty liars," Franklin said with a tight right fist.

J.L.'s eyes moistened almost imperceptibly as he continued, "With all the bravery in every war since the Civil War. With all the success. Just before I gets my black ass there they disbanded the 24th. Disbanded the best fighting outfit in Korea. So I get assigned to a demolition group."

"Was that part of your training?" Greg asked naively.

After looking at Greg like he was crazy J.L. continued, "Now, I'm the only Black guy in the troop. Guess who they make do all the really dangerous stuff? My comrades in arms gave me these Claymores. I'd never been up close to one of those before. They take my M-16 and tell me to go out there and plant them in the hard ground. They figured 'what's one more dead nigger' planting something.

So all the while I'm burying these mines by myself and positioning 'm just so, I'm dreaming of putting one under the Captain's bunk. I can just see him tumbling out of bed, putting his funky white feet in his shower shoes, and KaBoom!

But that's not stockade time, that's tree lynching time. So I watched my back and by the grace of God I made it out of there in one piece. The minute my time was up I got out and joined the Air Force."

"Praise God. Has the Air Force been any better?" Chap asked.

"Actually, it has. Eleven more months and I retire. But really, even being here with you and most of your Spam-eatin' posse has been a blessing to me. I do kind of hate to go back home to all that fighting. The fight is almost out of me."

"Really?" Greg asked.

"I said almost. You do not want to test me."

Franklin smiled for the second time.

CHAPTER 4

Shepherd Air Force Base

Wichita Falls, Texas

July 1966

Greg and Chap met for the first time at Shepherd AFB. Greg had been assigned there after basic for medic training. After graduating, many of the other medics were sent on to duty stations including Vietnam. Because Greg had shown a certain aptitude he was kept at Shepherd for additional training to become a surgical tech and work in the operating room.

None of this meant much to Greg because he thought he would soon be behind a camera covering the victims of war, not caring for them.

Saturdays during this second phase of training, airman were allowed to go into town. Town held a lot for young men away from home and girlfriends for the last six months. Greg was sure the people of Wichita Falls were decent people but they did not act like it during his time there.

That summer it was close to or over 100 degrees every day. Being from Houston, Greg preferred the heat to the bone chilling winters he heard about from others stationed there year round. He also heard of airmen on Saturday leave who had gotten "off base" and spent their Saturday nights in the Wichita County jail. Parents with daughters were rightly concerned. However, just because each airman wore a uniform did not mean every airman acted in uniformity. But still, it was Saturday and it was off base. A double-dipped cone from a cute, unparented daughter with great eyes and a sweet smile was plenty to combat a couple of harsh looks from residents on the street.

Sundays were a different story all together. During basic they marched to services on Sunday. For the first few at Shepherd, Greg took a sabbatical from the Christian Sabbath in church. He was free to do whatever he wanted as long as what he wanted was inside the fence of the base. But there were a lot of choices. Instead of a barracks full of guys, at Shepherd Greg was assigned a two-man room. Greg's roomie was there for one full day and then got heatstroke from playing basketball in the afternoon Texas sun. A replacement roommate was not assigned for several weeks so for a brief time, far unlike the experience of anyone in any service under the rank of captain, Greg had his own private room. He was even able to rent a small TV. Life was as good as it gets for a young man who was being trained to stop the hurting in a world of hurt.

But as Greg would find, old habits and new friends die hard. Come Sunday he began thinking about Trinity Street Baptist, Mountainview, and Melinda.

Not knowing the chapel schedule the first time he went, Greg walked in on a Greek Orthodox service with four others and the priest. Greg was surprised by the beauty and solemnity of the service. He wondered if Mrs. Dehartman was looking down thinking he was going to hell for not being in a Baptist service. This thought was followed by *Well, if she's looking down after having looked around up there, she's probably seen a lot that surprised her.* But he did check out the schedule for the Baptist's services for the following week.

The next Sunday Greg did come back for the Baptist service. He was surprised that the preacher conducting the service was a Black man not much older than himself. Greg had never worshipped with anyone Black, let alone been led by one. The guy could sing and not surprisingly, his congregation was almost a hundred times the size of the Greek Orthodox service. The mostly young, Black airmen jumped to their feet and begun clapping and singing along as soon as the music started. These were uncomfortable activities for Greg. An up-tempo "I'll Fly Away" was about as "getting down" as Trinity Street got. And a member had to just have had their one-hundredth birthday for applause to ever happen during a service. Clapping in church was about as hell-bent as, heaven forbid, drums.

Greg stayed seated for the first song but then got up and tried to clap in rhythm with the others. He soon gave up and tried Jack the Baptist's old trick of mouthing "Watermelon, watermelon" for a bit until he realized that wasn't the best fake lyrics at this moment.

Greg thought the music was great if a little long, but nothing like the length of the sermon. Greg and the old guys back home could have driven to Galveston and back for coffee and chocolate milk before this guy was through. The preacher did say a couple of things that seemed almost worth it but then with over three hundred black airmen and officers, in one of the worst towns in Texas, the preacher starts in on racial bias. *Oh crap*, Greg thought to himself. The large woman next to him, probably a visiting mom of one of the airmen, got excited. She started unknowingly flailing her arms and even punched Greg in the ribs once. Being the only Anglo in the room, Greg tried to assume an albino brother posture but even he wasn't buying that. He just sank back into his wooden pew and hoped the other troops were not imagining him wearing a white hood.

When Greg entered the sanctuary the usher sat him mid-way down the aisle next to the kind-looking woman with an oversized flowery hat and a very used Bible. It never occurred to him she could throw a mean Rosie Grier quarterback sack with a little encouragement from the pulpit Vince Lombardi.

Greg was wishing he had sat in the back like all good Baptists so he could slip out with few noticing. But if he got up from where he was seated and walked out, it could appear to be a sign of disrespect or fear. Neither message Greg cared about delivering, so he sat up tall and listened with his boots on.

Greg had only heard one side of this message before. He did not like the preacher's take although Greg had considered a couple of things before. Things like, if you separate students and then give those students an inferior education and then you have those students become teachers to teach the next generation of separated students, the outcome is pretty predictable.

But that had been corrected. In the halls of Greg's high school still walked jocks, and nerds, and bullies but now they were all colors. That had been fixed. So what was this guy going on about and why in a church? A church is the gateway to Jesus, friends, girls and chocolate milk, not loud complaining.

"And now before I close," the preacher said. *Crap again*, Greg thought. *If he recognizes visitors I'm not standing. They all know I'm a visitor. One who is definitely not returning.*

But it wasn't visitor recognition; it was "the plate." *Crap*, Greg thought for the third time. *I only have two dollars.* He had planned to use that for greens fees after tomorrow's training.

Shepherd AFB had a good golf course and it only cost one dollar to play, 50 cents for a couple of balls and only another 50 cents to rent clubs.

The silver plate seemed to sail down the aisles like a holy Frisbee. The fired-up Rosie Grier mom took all the change she had out of her purse and it hit the bottom of the plate like a Vegas slot machine paying off. Then she swung the offering plate with a "pay-up or die" look to Greg. Greg started to pass it on to the usher standing on his left but then Greg looked up at the stained glass Jesus and thought about home. His mother or Jack the Baptist had always given Greg a dime or a quarter to put in the plate. There was something "cool" about the event. Especially cool because it wasn't his golf money.

Greg did not like being pressured to do anything. But no matter how much he struggled and how much the usher coughed, Greg could not, not put in the two dollars. *Maybe I'll try reading a book*, Greg thought.

Greg was starving by the time the service ended and he hoped the chow hall was still serving lunch. Not knowing what to say to the minister, and with his stomach growling, Greg ducked the "shaking hands" line and went out the Emergency exit with total conviction that this emergency suited the sign perfectly. Greg headed straight for the mess hall as he left the base chapel and future services behind.

Greg never saw that Black chaplain again until Vietnam. Between the "whites only" Sears water fountains and Vietnam, names had changed. Colored became Negro, and Negro became Black. The Air Force did not allow Greg to wear a Beatles' haircut or sideburns. Franklin could not wear a "fro," but the rules about hair service-wide had loosened since the early Army Air Force years. In Vietnam, airmen could get away with a lot. All you had to do was risk your life every hour or so.

Greg couldn't believe it when he saw the same

Black preacher from Shepherd, standing over a wounded soldier in Greg's care.

"Let me by, Preacher," Greg said.

"It's not that bad," the Shepherd AFB preacher said. "They call me Chap."

Greg worked quickly on the soldier as he handed his flashlight to the chaplain. Chap followed Greg's movements with the greenish glow of the filtered light. Greg pointed and handed a sulfur stick, bandages, and tape to the Chaplain. Chap took the items and the two worked like an experienced team of jugglers on *The Hollywood Palace*.

"You're pretty good," Chap said.

"Thanks, you too," Greg responded.

"You're doing the hard part."

"No, I meant as a preacher. I heard you at Shepherd."

"The White Guy!" Chap said with instant clarity. The patient moaned.

"Shhh," Greg whispered.

"Sorry. I remember you. I wanted to talk to you afterward but you ducked out," Chap whispered.

"Shouldn't you be praying or something?" Greg asked.

"I stayed prayed ahead for all of this every day,"

Chap said.

Greg swabbed off the betadine he had used to clean the soldier's skin around the wound, never noticing the young soldier was darker than Chap.

CHAPTER 5

Somewhere in New Mexico

April 3, 1968

Greg stood in the updraft of a woman smoking a Virginia Slim. He had been on his feet in his dress shoes from Phoenix to Lordsburg, New Mexico. They had told him not to wear his Air Force uniform once he was back in the States, but Greg did not believe them. The Continental bus was crowded with Mexicans and children, old ladies, and a few servicemen who stayed uniformed as well. He stood there with his left arm in the strap like a kid with a circus balloon. In his right hand was a gym bag that contained a couple of things including Chap's manuscript. Having to deal with the bag made Greg wish he had checked it along with his duffel. New travelers stared at the standing sergeant. However, the stares would have been angry glares had Greg taken a seat and left a civilian standing.

Greg tried to pass the time and get his mind off his aching feet by repeating Roy Orbison lyrics in his head. She and Greg loved Roy Orbison. They had watched him on Ed Sullivan the night she put Greg's high school ring on a chain long enough to fall into her top to keep her father from asking questions. It did not keep Greg from wanting to reach in to get it whenever they were alone.

"In Dreams" danced through in his mind amidst the haze generated by the fog machine of his fellow riders cigarette puffing. The lyrics brought images. His first date with Melinda, their first kiss, sudden flashes of blood and open wounds, smells of wet plaster casts and Melinda's neck while they danced close, hiding and trying to stifle give-away laughter after almost being caught by her father when they weren't supposed to be seeing each other, Melinda's lips and then back to the lyrics,

> *Only in dreams*
> *In beautiful dreams.*

Dreams in the Delta were mostly nightmares. New in-country medics would eventually approach Greg about getting them something for the night terrors that were so prevalent. Along with Greg's surgical duties he also had access to surgical supplies, which included anesthetics and hard drugs like morphine. Darvon 64 was big. Soldiers would get a handful and take out the little BB inside and down the pills with a little Jack and be "in dreams" in no time. Downing "stuff" kept Greg's Dong Tam O.R. busy with shot-off toes and other "accidental" injuries.

By the time the dusty Continental road train

rolled into Lordsburg, Greg's thighs were aching from skiing forward when the bus slowed and surging backward when it sped up. Greg was glad to stretch his already stretched legs and sit at the counter of the greasy pie palace that was this stop's singular choice for food. The plastic covered menu was an artist's palette of after dinner condiments, greasy fingerprints and what could have been icing from an Italian Cream cake. Inside the plastic was a hand-typed "Specia s of the Day." The old typewriter that typed the menus appeared to have a missing "L." This was confirmed in Greg's mind when he read down and saw that the rib sandwich came with "co es aw".

Greg only had a few dollars left for the trip. He decided to just have coffee and a glazed donut. A large Marine sat on the next stool. They each made a half-inch nod in the other's direction, but said nothing. Greg knew that if he asked the Marine how it was going, he would say "fine," which would be the first lie. This would lead to another or, worse, the truth. If Greg was going to stand the next leg of the ride from Lordsburg to Las Cruces, he did not want to do it buddy-carrying any of the emotional items from the backpack of a Marine heading home.

A grizzled old soul in a hunting cap with flaps walked up behind Greg and the Marine, put a boney arm around Greg and moved him slightly clock-wise.

"Would you two look at that," old boney arms Pezzed his head toward a young hippie-looking couple at a table near the window.

"You boys over there while these two cutie-pies pick flowers and get high on peyote. It makes me sick at my stomach."

Sure it's not the Special? Greg wanted to say but did not want to encourage the old bigot.

The hippie man turned toward the three at the counter. Boney-arm stepped behind Greg and the Marine.

"Yeah, I'm talking about you, pot head. Why don't you-"

"GUS, YOUR CHILI OMELET'S GETTIN' COLD."

"'Bout time Lois. A guy could starve around here," old Boney-arm replied.

Gus shuffled back to his chili omelet with extra onions and beans. He never once thanked either Greg or the Marine for their service. But at this point a "thanks" would have surprised them both. Neither Greg nor his stool mate reacted.

"Air Force, huh?" the Marine asked. Greg nodded. "We say 'Semper Fi'. What do you guys say?"

"Duck!" Greg said with a straight face.

One gold tooth surrounded by a choir of white teeth made an appearance just as the waitress set a club sandwich in front of the Marine.

During the Viet Nam "conflict," guys Greg's age had several choices: go to college and keep going long enough to ride out the war, become a policeman, join the Peace Corps, leave for Canada, get drafted, or enlist. Greg had chosen to go to college. But as a freshman, Greg had made two mistakes: he didn't study and he didn't fall out of love.

Another man, this one in a too-hot-for-Lordsburg-New Mexico-suit and Montgomery Ward tie approached the two uniformed counter-sitters. There were parts of the country where there were still rules against someone of the Marine's skin color sitting at a counter. But Greg figured there was no part of the country where that rule would have been pointed out to this giant Marine.

"Excuse me," Too-hot-suit and tie interrupting nothing said. "You boys been there?" he asked quietly.

The Marine was not fond at all of the term "Boy" but let it go this time.

"Vietnam, I mean," Too-hot explained.

"I have. You?" Greg asked the Marine.

"Second tour," Marine said.

An uncomfortable Too-hot continued, "Well my boy Kenneth - would you like to see a picture of him in his uniform?"

"Seen a lot of uniforms," Marine said.

"The bus is going to be pulling out and…" Greg

added.

"Of course. I'm sorry to bother you but Kenneth just left for there - we had some difficulty with - but we're still family regardless and – Is it going to be bad for him?"

"What's his MOS?" Greg saw the confusion on his face and followed with, "Is he in the Army?"

"Marines, like him, only white. That was a stupid thing to say. I'm sorry. It's just that his Mother and I are so-"

"I'm sure he will be fine. Look at us. We're both heading home and we're fine," Greg encouraged as he concealed his lie and was pretty sure he was lying for the Marine as well.

"Yeah, and Charlie's not supposed to light up any white Marines. I'm sure it's in the contract he signed," the Marine said with a straight face.

"Okay. Thanks. You boys got parents at home? I am sure they are very proud," Too-hot added.

"Thank you but we really have to finish-"

"Of course, sorry," Too-hot said walking away not even offering to pay for their food.

"If the kid is anything like his old man he's probably already in a body bag," the Marine said with the dark humor of war. The Marine tore off a hunk of his BLT between his gold-tooth smile.

The waitress put Greg's glazed donut in front of him. It was cold, which was okay with Greg, but he did wonder why it took longer to bring a cold donut than a club sandwich on toast. The waitress reached across the counter with the dirty coffee carafe to re-fill Greg's coffee cup just as Greg started to dunk his donut. When the coffee pot collided with Greg's donut hand the bad timing shot hot java across the sticky green Formica countertop. The tsunami of sugar, cream and Folger's cascaded off the counter and headed directly for the Marine's uniform slacks.

With lightening reflexes the Marine jumped off his stool. His gold tooth no longer showed. The waitress swooped in with a dirty dishcloth but instead of damming up the coffee, she hockey-pucked Greg's donut, coffee cup, and remaining hot coffee into Greg's lap. Greg did not have the Marine's reflexes.

Before she could say she was sorry, the bus driver stood at the door and announced the bus's immediate departure. The waitress ripped Greg's ticket from her pad, held it in Greg's direction, and then said, "That's okay hon. Forget about it." Greg would have loved to have forgotten about it if his steaming boxers weren't suddenly forged to his right thigh. Grabbing his gym bag, Greg limped out the door and onto the steps of the bus. The old bus driver examined Greg's broad wet spot and said, "Don't worry 'bout it. When you get my age, happens all the time."

The good news was that there were enough

seats for everyone to sit on the next leg to Las Cruces. After all the events at the diner Greg was not sleepy. He sat there in the sticky trousers and decided to finally start Chap's book. He had not been able to bring himself to read it up until now. The marine in uniform, the questions, the people; it all somehow reminded Greg of his friend. Maybe reading his words would help his sudden aloneness. Greg unzipped his gym bag, moved boxers and medic whites aside and uncovered the three-inch thick pile of paper. There was enough daylight to read by. The sleeping rider in the window seat next to Greg adjusted toward his window, leaving Greg more room to get comfortable to begin. Across the aisle sat a sweet little girl and her mother. Greg thought that they were probably on their way to see Grandma. The little girl smiled at Greg and he smiled back. Maybe he and Melinda would have a little girl like that one day. One day after having Greg the Third, of course. The little girl looked back at Greg again with Chap's manuscript in his hand.

"Look Mommy," she said, "that man wet his pants like Joshie." The bus laughed. That was it! He forced Chap's manuscript into the seat pocket in front of him, picked up his gym bag and headed for the latrine.

Just as Greg reached for the small door handle of the onboard bathroom, the door flashed open and the small entire portal filled with the Marine. Still no sign of the gold tooth and white choir. He stepped past Greg into the aisle, and Greg entered and locked the small door lock. While it was apparent the club-sandwiched-Marine had been in there, it was nothing compared to the odors Greg had endured in and out of his operating room in the Mekong.

Greg removed his wet khaki pants and boxers. After a quick wash and fresh underwear from his bag, Greg started to work on the coffee stain and sugar-glazed bullseye the waitress left on his military lap. He had a small brush that he would use to scrub his pre-surgical nails and hands all the way to his elbows. He had wrapped the brush in an autoclaving towel along with a couple of hemostats, a scalpel and a few other small "souvenirs" he brought back with him. The brush with some soap on it was ideal for this road-rolling laundry. With the hard bristled brush and lots of elbow grease the stain lightened. Now it was no longer a sugary, dark khaki-colored wet spot. It was simply a larger dark khaki-colored wet spot that Greg hoped would dry before Houston.

He rolled the wet slacks in the towel and twisted. Nothing really happened. He unrolled the towel, took out the pants and whipped them in the air hard like a matador's cape. The popping noise of the action sounded like progress but the wet spot was going to be there for a long time yet. Greg lowered the pants to the floor and just before he stuck his right foot in, he noticed the small, jalousie bathroom window to the outside. Panel breaks in the quarter inch thick glass slats of the window were about four inches apart. Greg rotated the tiny crank that opened the slats enough to see fence posts whizzing by. Desperate for quick

results, he stuffed his wet pants between two of the
parted panes of frosted glass. Once on the other side
of the window, the pants unfurled like the flag on a
battleship.

Greg held tight to the quick drying pants. It was
working, he convinced himself. When he thought they
had had enough exposure to the wind and hot desert
sun, Greg changed his grip to pull them back inside.
Suddenly a banging at the bathroom door synced with a
huge gust of New Mexico wind and the gauntlet-
traveled pants ripped from Greg's fist and went
airborne. Greg's left eye went to the opening in the
window but they had kited off like a Benjamin Franklin
experiment. Another bang on the door and Greg
unlocked it to see the mother and his disowned
daughter needing to get in. With one uncomfortable
revolution, they were in and Greg was out. The door
opened again and the mother handed Greg his gym
bag.

Greg rushed down the aisle toward the driver
until a scream from an older woman traveler reminded
him he was wearing only his shirt, boxers and dress
shoes. In the aisle he quickly pulled his medic whites
out and did a reverse striptease before continuing his
rush to the driver.

"Son, I ain't stopping this bus. I am late now,"
the bus driver said.

"But my wallet and discharge orders are in

those pants. We have to go back." Greg hadn't even thought of all of that until he said it.

"I'm sorry, I not supposed to even let you talk to me. See that sign? But I'll tell you what I will do." Air brakes sounded and Greg was hurled into the small foxhole by the bus's front accordion door.

Somewhere on a New Mexico highway, Staff Sergeant Gregory "Greg" Wofford Henderson, Jr., Serial Number 607-90-1112, began his 100-degree force-marched recon for pants as his bus roared off.

Putting one dust-covered, spit-shined shoe in front of the other at noon in the land of the Apache, was different from the screen glamour of Clint Eastwood's desert walk in *The Good, the Bad and the Ugly*. The dry New Mexico air was also very different from the humid, breezeless, hot vapor of the Delta on the day they were hit.

CHAPTER 6

Somewhere in the Delta

South Vietnam

October 12, 1967

Sergeants Parks and Harris were with Greg. Lt. Forsythe was their young resident. One of the wonders of war was that the enlisted medics and "lifers" were much more experienced than the doctor officers. Many young resident surgeons drank to calm the fear, took uppers to not cut an artery, and downers to forget the blood and get a little sleep.

One surprising thing about hospital surgeries is the lack of blood. The blood keeps you from seeing the tissues you need to fix or remove. So "Doc" officers and enlisted techs suctioned out the blood into sterilized tubing that led into a sterilized jar. The only sounds heard were the occasional beep of a monitor, the vacuum nozzle trapped against an organ, and the orders of the surgeon. There would be a little blood on the swabs in the jaws of a clamped hemostat, but very little blood elsewhere, even on the latex gloves of the surgeon.

But not that day. Lt. Forsythe's gloved hands and arms were elbow-deep dark with fresh red blood covering already dried blood from other young patients.

Greg and the other two surgical techs were covered, as well. Arterial wounds sprayed at them like lawn sprinklers. There was no time to feel sorry, cry, or be scared. But fear made a way.

Greg could not believe Chap had made it there alive. The firefight was the hottest Greg had seen. Their triage was set up only yards behind the two well-armed forces. Chap crawled into a clearing, stopping at each wounded soldier to pray.

"What can I do?" Chap asked Greg when he finally reached him. Greg was starting IVs as Sgt. Parks worked on a gaping stomach wound.

"You seen any Choppers?" Greg asked Chap. Chap shook his head and asked, "They on their way?"

"Hope so," Greg said as he moved to a wounded PFC. And then it happened. One zing hit the ground near the PFC. A second shattered the IV bottle of Dextrose Greg held in his hand. The shards of glass slow-motioned in all directions. Greg hit the ground, but Chap beat him to it. Greg raised his head above safety to try to determine the enemy's location. "We have to get behind those sandbags."

Greg, for the first time since he was sworn-in in Houston, drew his sidearm.

"C'mon," Greg told Chap. Greg ran through the zings and slid into third behind his "unit one pack", a backpack the combat medics carried. Chap was on his heels. Greg crawled back to check on the PFC and saw he was dead. He ran back to the sanctuary of the sandbags. On the ground was a new helmet with an Ace of Hearts stuck in its olive green elastic band. Three yards from the helmet was the young surgical resident. His Lieutenant brass was still shiny. Greg knew if the Lieutenant was dead, he would have to do any surgical procedures alone. But suddenly the Lieutenant stirred. He had blood over his right eyebrow and when he regained consciousness, he thought he was blind. Chap calmed him as the zings from the firefight slowed to a few distant "pops." Greg laid his .38 special sidearm on one of the sandbags as he cleaned the skull wound of the Lieutenant. Soon the Lieutenant realized he could see. Another miracle out of the carnage. But before they could celebrate, a shadow of one of Charlie's finest appeared out of nowhere. Greg reached for his Beretta and fired all in one motion. The enemy soldier emptied his clip all around Chap, the Lieutenant, and Greg before dotting the clouds with his last rounds.

"Get back!" Greg yelled as Chap rushed to the soldier. Greg, with his sidearm still smoking, reached Chap as he stared at the lifeless soldier. Around the dead young VC's neck was the cross the young villager had made for Chap. Chap gently removed the cross and prayed over the short-lived life of the young boy. Greg threw his sidearm in the brush as hard as he could.

Chap caught up with Greg that night. Greg was sitting beside the surgical tent staring at a wallet picture of Melinda. He never really wanted to be there, but for the first time all kinds of plots for escape ran through his mind.

"You can't just go throwing government property around like this," Chap said as he handed Greg his sidearm.

"You keep it," Greg said.

"It might help at that. Those Sunday offerings have been down quite a bit lately." Chap twirled the Beretta around his index finger and then dropped it to the ground.

"If you're going to play with it at least put the safety on," Greg suggested.

Both men sat quietly for a while.

An MP walked by on his way to guard duty. "Hey Padre. Hey Doc," he called out.

Both men returned his greeting.

After a bit more silence Chap asked, "I ever tell you about my book?"

"Book?" Greg asked.

Chap nodded. "Well a manuscript, it's never been published. Is the Lieutenant okay?"

"Yeah, he'll be fine. Pretty close call, though."

"Thank God for miracles," Chap said earnestly.

"You prayed ahead for miracles too?" Silence. "Wished you had prayed more for that kid I killed today," Greg said.

"For better aim? Then who would I be out here under God's moon with?"

Silence.

"How many lives you think you have saved?" Chap asked.

"Me? No way of knowing. We patch them up as good as we can and send them off to Clark or somewhere."

"Right."

"You trying to say that if I save more than I kill, God will be okay with that?" Greg questioned.

"Did you hear me say that? I was just trying to think of something more positive."

"Trying to keep people alive around here is like eating soup with a toothpick."

"What?"

"Oh, just something my Grandmother used to say about anything that takes forever or is futile."

"Tell me about her," Chap said gesturing to Melinda's picture. Greg and Chap were war-close, death-close, miracle-close but not Melinda-close.

"Not now. Tell me about this Best Seller you are writing."

"I'm not sure you really want to know about it."

"Why? You writing dirty books under a pen name?"

"Some people might think it's pretty dirty all right."

"Reverend Peyton Place, the Casanova Chaplain. That would look good on a dust jacket."

"If you'll shut up, I'll tell you about it."

"All right. What's it called?"

"The Curse of Ham and Grits."

"Cook book? Sounds like a recipe for disaster."

"You sound like the publishers I talked to," Chap said.

"Okay I'll stop. Tell me about it."

Chap said. "You were raised Baptist, right?"

"Yeah, I guess."

"And in the South?"

"Texas. Not the South." Greg corrected.

"Which side was Texas on in the Civil War?"

"Did you write a textbook? Do I get college

credit for answering you? The South, okay. Texas fought with the South."

"And lost." Chap jabbed a bit.

"Yes. What does that have to do with your curse?"

"Well the curse of Ham is what a bunch of you losers used as an excuse for keeping slaves."

"I never had a slave. I had a Robbie the Robot."

"You remember Noah? I bet you used a different crayon for each one of the animals. You probably had the 16 color box."

"48 count."

"Including Flesh?" Chap asked.

"Yeah, that's right. Flesh was in there. Kind of pinkish like."

"So, Noah had three sons. Remember their names?"

"Sure, there was Shem," Greg said to Chap's surprise. "Curly and Noah, junior." Chap was no longer surprised.

"How old were you when you were saved?"

"Twelve. Want to hear all the books of the Bible in order?"

"Then you were baptized?"

"Well…"

"You haven't been baptized?"

"Well, I was going to be baptized. But then I remembered the thief on the Cross."

"Go on," Chap prodded.

"Well, Jesus said the thief would be with Him in Paradise and he wasn't baptized. The thief, I mean."

"So, let me get this straight, with all the heroes of the Bible you learned about as a child, the one you identified with was the thief on the Cross?"

"Let's get back to your book," Greg redirected.

"Noah had three sons-"

"Da da da Da. Da da da Da. You ever watch *My Three Sons?* What can I say? I'm incorrigible. I admit it. But c'mon anybody would be thinking of that theme song with that set up. "

Chap decided at this point to press right through any more comments. He had never really shared any part of his book one-on-one before. The fact he was doing it with a white boy sitting on a banana leaf in the middle of South Vietnam did not escape Chap's sense that irony sharpens irony. But he had gotten to a point where he had a strong need share this work with someone. In Vietnam his book was becoming a far off vision. He needed to bring it back into his sense of present reality. If he shared it with Franklin/Abidemi or J.L. they would get too fired up and get him off track. For some strange reason Chap trusted Greg more than any other man in his life. He hoped this was a God thing.

Chap pressed on, "After the flood Noah planted a vineyard. From the vineyard he took grapes."

"Oh yeah, this is where Noah gets wasted and lies around naked."

"Good. That's right, sort of. You know what happens next?"

"Of course--- but why don't you tell me. It's your book." Greg had no clue.

"You ever see a nigger-hanging?" Chap asked coldly.

Greg's smile vanished immediately. "What?"

"Did....you...ever....see...a Black man swinging from the limb of a tree? His coveralls all wet in the front 'cause he peed himself before he died."

Greg got very quiet.

"If you happened upon such a thing at night would you think that was a man or a pig? I have seen you with your whole arms inside a Black soldier. Anything in there look different to you? Without the shrapnel was his liver in the same place? Was his stomach in the same place, even with the punji sticks? Was his heart in the same place?"

Greg was taken aback by Chap sudden harshness. "You've seen Black soldiers with parts of their skulls missing. Did their remaining skull look any different? Did their brain look any different to you?"

Chap took a breath now that all was quiet. "Well there were men, good men in their own way, who thought that we were different. Physically, emotionally, spiritually."

"How?" Greg asked.

"The Big Lie goes like this-"

"The Curse you mean?" Greg tried to keep up.

"Right. And this part is true. That's what is so insidious about using the Bible to support your own agenda. You start with the truth. Noah got drunk. His son Ham comes in and sees his father laying there naked in this drunken stupor. Instead of covering him up and letting him sleep it off, Ham makes fun of his father. Now the other two other sons, Shem and Japheth, hear about their father's embarrassing condition and go to him. Because children are not supposed to see their father naked they back into the room and cover him up.

Hung-over, Noah wakes up. He hears about Ham's disrespect and jokes, and here's where the lies start, puts an irreversible curse on Ham. Now, under the curse Ham and all his descendants are to be servants to Shem and Japheth. Ham's heirs eventually settled in Africa. So the story is told these descendants simply wait there in Africa until European ships bring cloth and shiny things to trade for Ham's grandchildren so that these tribesmen get to go, all expenses paid, to America to fulfill their Noah-cursed and God-approved assignment to serve the white descendants of Shem and Japheth."

"How do you know that's a lie?" Greg asks.

"If you read the Bible, Noah's curse was put on Canaan, one of Ham's four sons, not Ham. Noah spoke the curse, not God, and God is not responsible for the curses of a drunk. If that were true I would have been sent to Hell a long time ago. Canaan's descendants dominated Palestine for seventeen centuries. Not much of a curse."

"So, that's what your book is about?" Greg asked.

"Some of it," Chap answered. He then got to his feet and said to Greg, "Let's go."

Greg got up and followed. "I hope they have ham tonight. For some reason I'm in the mood..." Chap stopped Greg, Greg thought maybe his last comment went over the line.

"Wait," Chap cautioned.

"What? What did you hear? VC?" Greg touched his returned sidearm.

"This way." Chap smiled slightly and led.

"Where are we going?" Greg asked.

"Just follow me and keep quiet."

Every step took the pair deeper in mud.

"Halt," commanded the sentry right out of a John Wayne movie. "You two lost? Go on back to camp. It's that way," directed the young soldier.

"I'm on assignment." Chap said to the soldier.

"Okay, Padre. Just be careful."

"It's all right," Greg explained, "He stays prayed ahead."

The young sentry looked confused but satisfied.

"If you keep going we're going to run into the river." Greg said.

Chap didn't stop. Greg now thought he knew what was happening.

"C'mon Chap. This is really not necessary. I mean I've gone all these years. God's probably okay with it by now."

Chap halted like he had seen seasoned soldiers do on the parade ground. Chap turned to Greg in the sparse light of the fingernail moon and faced him close, Drill Sergeant close.

"There is death and destruction all around us. Do you really want to meet God and tell Him face-to-face that you knew you were supposed to do this to show your commitment, but... you didn't want to get your hair wet?"

Chap didn't wait for an answer. He spun on his heels and continued on in the muddier and muddier sod until they reached the My Tho. Once the two made it to the riverbank, Chap just kept on walking in until the water was just below waist high. When he turned back to the bank, Greg was standing there. Chap didn't say anything; he just reached out his hand. Chap knew from conversations and his actions that Greg's early commitment was intentional. He left everything else between Greg and God. If this was to be a late night dip in a murky Vietnamese river, that was okay, too. Chap felt he was acting out his calling and cared for the "afraid-of-water white guy hesitating on the bank," the way one brother cares for another.

Greg inched into the water. He didn't take Chap's offered hand, but sloshed and then waded waistdeep. "You know how many things in this water could kill us?" Greg asked as he moved in front of Chap .

"Do you not want to do this?" Chap returned.

"No, I mean yes, I do. Let's get this done before I decide sprinkling is the way to go."

Chap raised his right hand toward God's moon and said, "By your profession of faith those many years ago and your continued walk toward Jesus,"

"Wait," Greg stopped him wanting to set the record straight.

"Shut up," said the knowing Chaplain as he supported the taller Greg with his left hand behind his neck and placed Greg's hands over his nose with his right. "I baptized thee." Greg was suddenly under the murky waters of the My Tho for what seemed like thirty seconds when suddenly tiny projectiles were zinging through the water.

Chap's grip on Greg was hard and fast. Greg struggled to release Chap's grip and get a foothold on the slick silt bottom of the My Tho. Finally, Greg tore Chap's hand away. When he broke the surface gasping, he was behind the floating body of his chaplain friend. Chap had been hit with multiple rounds. Greg pulled Chap's floating body behind the banana leaves along the bank. A couple of drunk enemy soldiers were firing at a log floating down the river and probably didn't even know they had wounded this man of God in the performance of his duty. As the soldiers stumbled away, Greg got Chap to the bank. Even in the dim light Greg could tell Chap's wounds were bad. Everything was wet. Greg peeled off his shirt and made a pillow for Chap. Chap started to talk.

"We got you done." Chap said as he began to slip away.

"No, you're not. You're going to make it," Greg said.

"Prayed-"

"Prayed ahead, I know. Stay with me Chap," Greg whispered as loud as he could.

"My book," Chap said as his blood mixed with the wet clay of the bank.

"My BOOK!" Chap shouted.

"Shhh. Hang in there." Greg said as he threw his broken friendship over his shoulder.

Chap moaned in pain.

"I've got drugs Chap. Just a little farther. They'll stop the pain." Greg started to cry for the first time since that masked doctor slapped him. "Our Father who art in Heaven," Greg prayed anything he could think of through the tears.

"C'mon Chap, pray with me." Each friend-ladened, mud-bogged step was more challenging than the last.

"Hallowed be Thy name." Chap whispered in a bouncing cadence and then,

"MY BOOK! THEY HAVE TO SEE MY BOOK! THEY HAVE TO SEE-"

"They Will, I PROMISE CHAP. I PROMISE. Just stay with-"

The two drunken VC suddenly sprang from the bushes. Shots were fired. The young sentry put five shells each into the two drunks that murdered Chap.

"They got 'm Chap! Stay with me!" Greg, exhaustedly quieted to a near whisper, "Stay with me. The danger's over. We're safe. Stay with me-" Greg pleaded with the dead weight of his friend on his shoulders. Greg did not realize until an hour later that some of the blood on his fatigues was his own.

CHAPTER 7

New Mexico Desert

April 3, 1968

Cars zoomed by as Greg walked the desert highway. One or two even stopped to see if he needed a ride. Greg just thanked them. He was too embarrassed to say he was in the desert looking for his pants.

Then one older man stopped. Greg kept walking. The old man took his foot off the break and his car's idling pace rolled alongside Greg as he walked. The tires crunched shell and rock slowly as they turned.

"You lost, young feller?" The old man was wearing a new khaki Dickie work shirt and pants. His turquoise belt buckle was missing at least four stones. His straw hat had been doffed or waved or blown off so many times it was curled like a two week-old piece of bologna in Greg's old refrigerator. The old man's whiskers were sun-bleached and the knuckles on his right hand were still recovering from an accident or a fight.

"No, sir," Greg finally answered the question about being lost.

"Don't see many people out here who know where they are going," the old man offered. His words crawled out of his mouth like frozen honey. Greg figured to himself he could find his pants and be in the next town before this slow motion version of *What's My Line* was over.

"Well, I don't really know where I'm going," Greg continued walking.

"You know where you are?" The old man punched his accelerator and got a few feet ahead of Greg.

"Not really," Greg said. The old man pulled his car beyond the shoulder and threw it into park while it was still rolling. The action caused the car to lurch and sputter. The sputter continued a few more seconds after the ignition was turned off. The door creaked open and a dusty Tony Lama left boot planted in the sand.

"You don't know where you're going and you don't know where you are, but you aren't lost?"

"I'm not lost... my pants are."

The Good Septuagenarian drove nothing like he talked. Once Greg and his gym bag were aboard, the old man's Mercury took off like a bat out of Carlsbad Caverns. The old man reached across Greg's lap, popped his glove compartment door, and pulled out what appeared to be a brown liquid in a labeless bottle. In the glove compartment, Greg saw a Luger and a bunch of odd shaped fishing weights. The man grabbed the cork between his right molars and twisted until the bottle popped free. When he spit out the cork at Greg's feet, his upper dentures went with it. Greg started to reach down for them on the Mercury's sandy floorboard, but stopped.

"Want a snort?" the old man asked.

"No thanks. A little hot and early."

"Man in uniform turning down a drink? No wonder we're…"

"No wonder we're what?"

"No wonder we're getting our butts kicked."

"Stop the car," Greg ordered.

"You spot your pants?"

"No. Just stop the car."

"What is this, a date?"

"Look, you old drunk. Stop the car and let me out or…"

"Or what? You gonna get your hippie friends to love me to death? I thought I was helping out a soldier. I'm gonna take you out here and beat the quitter out of you."

The denture less old man steered the car roughly off the road again and slid to a stop between several tall cacti. Greg got out as the old man came around the front of the car with a Louisville Slugger.

The swoosh of the bat came close enough to Greg's head for him to hear the air. The suddenly deranged old fart started a backhanded swing; Greg blocked it and knocked the old man down with a strong left hook.

"You knocked out my teeth you son-of-a-. I hope a rattler, Gila monster, and tarantula suck the life out of you before you get out of here."

The old man got back in his car, holding his jaw, and started to drive off. His rear wheels spun in the sand. Greg thought about grabbing the bat and knocking out a headlight. Once the old man gained traction, the Mercury lurched forward. Instead of getting back on the blacktop, the old man turned the car and raced back toward Greg. Greg dodged the dinged up car as sand fishtailed behind it. Greg ducked behind a large cactus. The tail-finned, sand tank clipped spines off of it as it zoomed by. The old man spun the car again, threw it in low, sited Greg through his homemade hood ornament, and floored the gas pedal. Greg jumped out of the way moments before the old man's Merc slammed into the largest blooming century plant in that part of the dessert. The old man was thrown from the car on impact. He stretched out to reach the bat lying in the sand a few feet away before losing consciousness. Greg kicked the bat away and got his gym bag out of the car. He started to walk toward the highway. Twenty yards from the old man, Greg looked back at him lying in the hot shadow of the century plant.

As Greg knelt to check his pulse with his left hand, he kept his right fist cocked. "Crazies have super-human power," some of his medic friends that had worked in institutions before the Air Force told him.

The old man came around just as Greg was setting his shoulder. He moaned, swung at the air with his good arm, and passed out again. Greg dumped the old man in the backseat and then climbed behind the wheel. The Mercury's front end had surrounded the trunk of the century plant like a grandmother hugging her youngest. Greg put the chugging chariot in reverse and, after a moment, the car released its hug and started smoking as it backed up. Once cleared of the tree, Greg put the car in gear and then stopped. Stuck on several spines of a large cactus only thirty yards away were Greg's sandy dress pants. It wasn't until that eureka moment cleared his head that Greg suddenly remembered Chap's manuscript was still on the bus headed for Houston.

KEN BAILEY

CHAPTER 8

Just Outside Deming, New Mexico

April 3, 1968

The old cactus-killer slumped over onto Greg while Greg was trying to steer the damaged car. Greg shoved him off his shoulder, leaving the old guy's head wound sunbathing under the hot New Mexico sky.

Greg pulled into Deming aboard the smoking, limping Mercury. He drove up in front of an old, two-story, wooden hospital. Greg walked through a door marked "Emergency."

A young fellow with a stethoscope draped around his neck was sucking on a corndog. The young man in white scrubs with a small mustard stain felt the need to explain his eating choice.

"All I can find soft enough to try to eat. Wisdom teeth pulled. Hurts like- oww."

"You the doc here?" Greg asked.

"What'd you need?" slightly swollen beard-jaw asked.

"Got this old guy out in the car…" The doctor opened the screen door to get a better look.

"That's Mac Parker's car. What's he done now?"

Greg helped the young doctor get Mac Parker onto the examining table. "This is a pretty good job you did on the shoulder here. You a doctor?"

"No."

The Doc scanned Greg's odd mix of a khaki uniform shirt and white pants and said, "Oh, medic. Sorry, I should have noticed. I haven't gone in yet. Supposed to go in for six months during my surgery residency. I'll be a 2nd Lieutenant. Hoping Johnson or the next president ends it before I have to go. Hate to shave the beard. The ladies love it."

"Where can I catch a bus to Las Cruces around here?" Greg asked.

"Just out the door and over to the Cactus Cafe. Did you just find old Mac after he crashed?"

"Cactus Cafe?" Greg confirmed.

"Tell Lutrena I said fix you up. The hospital will pay for it."

"Thanks."

"You're welcome. Maybe I'll see you around the O.R. or mess hall or somewhere."

"You won't see me," Greg responded going out the door he entered.

Greg could smell the burnt grease of the deep-fryer almost a block away from the Cactus Cafe. True to its name, the café was full of cacti for sale. An atypical-looking waitress crossed to Greg. "Sit anywhere except on somebody." She was atypical-looking but not atypical- sounding. "You need a menu hon?"

"Yes, the doctor at the hospital told me to tell Lutrena to fix me up."

"Oh, he did, did he? Do I look like a Lutrena to you?"

The question took Greg aback.

"Well... I am." Lutrena laughed as she slapped the water glass down in front of Greg creating a small wading pool on the counter she did not bother to wipe up.

"Did you hear that one, Charlie?" Lutrena laughingly asked a fat guy in the corner. "One 'hospital special' coming up," as she walked away.

"Excuse me, what's the hospital special... Lutrena?"

"Two drumsticks on little crutches. Naw, I'm just funnin'. Did you hear that one Charlie?

Drumsticks on little crutches."

Turning back to Greg Lutrena explained, "It's really a grilled cheese on rye with potato chips," as she slapped down a bottle of Tabasco sauce on the table.

"What makes that the hospital special?"

"Cuz that's all the hospital will pay for."

"Could I get that on white bread instead of rye?"

"That's the Mayor's special. But we won't tell the hospital, will we Charlie?"

"I guess, you better not tell the Mayor either," Greg quipped, trying to play along.

"He already knows. Charlie there is the Mayor." Lutrena laughed as Charlie the Mayor hooked his thumbs under his suspender straps and stretched the elastic out as far away from his fat stomach as possible.

Minutes later Lutrena set the grilled cheese on rye with the tiny toothpick speared pickle slice down in front of Greg.

"Sorry, Charlie got the last two slices of white bread. Just spit out the seeds. It'll be fine."

"The doctor said this is the bus stop for Greyhound."

"Sure is, that's where all the rest of the white

bread went. If you were heading for Texas you just missed it. Not five minutes ago."

Discouraged, Greg pulled the toothpick out and started to take a bite of the hospital special.

"If I ain't mistaken," Mayor Charlie remarked, "That bus is stilling fillin' up over at Quincy's Esso.

Greg spun on his stool and went toward the window.

"Course, these windows are so greasy, it could be the Starship Enterprise," Mayor Charlie joked.

Through the glass Greg could see the tail end of a bus just over a block away.

Greg ran back to the counter, grabbed his gym bag and the rest of his grilled cheese and ran out the door.

"THE HOSPITAL DON'T TIP!" Lutrena yelled after him.

"Oh forget it, Lu, he's one of our fightin' boys," Mayor Charlie offered.

"Shut up Charlie or I'll come pop those suspenders myself."

"Okay, okay calm down. He ain't registered to vote here anyhow. You want me have Eugene stop the bus and get you a big tip?"

As Greg ran he saw the backup lights on the bus brighten. He heard the gears grind just as he reached the passenger side. Greg's left hand slapped the racing dog logo hard and the woman in the window above looked down to see what it was. She must have alerted the driver because within twenty feet the bus stopped, the door opened, and Greg jumped on. For a moment Greg looked down the long narrow aisle and saw no familiar faces. Panic set in as he considered the possibility he had stopped the wrong bus.

"You almost didn't make," the not-so-friendly but very familiar bus driver observed. "Where's your ticket?"

"I gave it to you in San Francisco when I got on." Greg reminded the surly driver.

"Oh yeah, the soldier with no pants."

Greg was going to correct the soldier thing but it wasn't worth it. The bus lunged away from the gas pumps making Greg have to grab onto the upper luggage racks to stay upright. Greg made his way back to his old seat and his worst fear was realized. Chap's manuscript was not where he left it.

Greg parallel-barred like a gymnast using the overhead bins back up to the driver.

"Did you see some papers back where I was sitting?" Greg asked.

The driver did not answer.

"Excuse me," Greg said again, "Did you see-"

The driver pointed to an overhead sign that read *Do Not Speak to the Bus Driver.*

"I don't want to CHAT. I simply want to know where my papers are!"

The bus blinker turned on and the driver pulled over onto the gravel shoulder ninety feet past the "You are leaving Deming" sign. Greg thought, *Oh crap, he's going to kick me off again.*

But instead, the bus driver turned to Greg and said, "Now, what are you talking about?

"C'mon, we're late," complained one of the many tired passengers.

"Do you want off here too?" the bus driver asked the heckler.

"A book. Actually just papers, clipped together with a big...?" Greg said.

"I've got a Louie L'Amour you can read after I go to the bathroom," another passenger offered.

"I don't need something to read, I NEED MY BOOK!" Greg vehemently shouted.

"Sorry, can't help you soldier," the bus driver said remounting his driver's seat. "Sit down and let me get these people where they're going or get off. Makes no never mind to me."

Having lost the chance to do the one thing he had promised his dying friend, Greg trudged back down the aisle to find a seat.

Suddenly the onboard bathroom door opened and hit the knee of an old woman on the very back row. The jolt caused the missing manuscript pages to slide downhill to her ample breast ski-lift, be launched skyward, and suspended in mid-air before sticking a landing on the gritty, rubber-matted, back of the bus floor.

Greg mumbled an instant prayer of thanksgiving as he rushed to reclaim the floored treasure.

"Hey! Where you going with my book? " the sweet, waking, grandmotherly type Black woman said with a Southern sheriff's tone.

Greg tried to briefly explain about his promise to Chap.

"But you ain't Black," the woman observed. "Why would a Black pastor.." she paused and looked Greg over, "ask a mess like you to get this book done for him?"

"I was all he had," Greg told her. The answer satisfied her.

"Well, okay, but when you get it done I want a copy." Greg borrowed a pen from a salesman in row Y and wrote down her name and address.

"You know, I read enough to know them Baptists gonna' hate you for this. And I don't mean my Baptists, honey." She laughed.

Relieved to have Chap's book back, Greg sat down and looked seriously at the cover of the promised creation. *When will I have this much time to read?* he thought. The typewritten title page simply read, "The Curse of Ham and Grits by Rev. Terrance L. Bonner." Greg turned the pages to "Chapter 1."

> ***America's largest Protestant denomination began by believing slavery was consistent with the Biblical teachings. This is the shameful story of Southern Baptists and the continuing fight for racial equality.***

"Oh crap!" Greg uttered out loud awakening his seatmate. "Sorry," he apologized to his fellow traveler who mumbled something incoherent and repositioned himself to go back to sleep.

Greg was sorry. Sorry for the promise he made without having a clue how to make it happen and sorry for the way this book could hurt people he cared about.

Oh Crap! This one he kept to himself. *Melinda's father!* He would never let her see Greg after this.

Maybe he was being overly concerned about

Chap's book. Chap was a great, caring pastor and
friend. How really controversial could his book be?
Greg continued to read.

> *Before the Southern*
> *Baptists contemplated chicken-fried*
> *suicide, all Baptist churches*
> *belonged to the General*
> *Convention of the Baptist*
> *Denomination in the United*
> *States for Foreign Missions.*

Greg thought their letterhead must have run
sideways.

> *…also known as the Triennial Convention.*

That wasn't bad.

> *There was a growing movement*
> *within the convention against slavery. The*
> *Georgia Baptists nominated a slave owner*
> *named James Reeve to be a missionary. His*
> *nomination was rejected by the Home*
> *Mission Board on the moral grounds of slave*
> *ownership. That rejection, along with other*
> *related events, drove the wedge of division*
> *deeper between Northern and Southern*
> *Baptists and soon Baptist life in the South*
> *would change forever.*

> *The tension continued to escalate.*
> *A prominent Baptist preacher*
> *Rev. Basil Manly, Sr., who*
> *himself owned 40 slaves, drafted*

*the "Alabama Resolutions". This
was a set of articles which
demanded that Baptist slave
owners who financially supported
the Convention be allowed to serve
as missionaries and at other posts.
When no encouraging response
came from the Northern Baptists,
the Southern Baptist Convention
was formed at First Baptist
Church Augusta, Georgia in May
of 1845.*

Okay, thought Greg. *A lot of groups have shaky
beginnings but the Southern Baptists did not become the church of
his childhood by continuing such un-Christian-like attitudes,
except maybe Jelly.*

Chap went on to write how some early Baptist
leaders employed the Curse of Ham theory that he had
explained to Greg back in the Delta. And other leaders
even used Paul's writings on the slave-master
relationship to reinforce their dogma. Chap said that
resolutions from the annual conventions gave insight
into the tensions within and without.

Resolution on Colored People

Baltimore, Maryland - 1868

*RESOLVED, 3rd. That we
believe that the time has fully come
for the introduction of a new
instrumentality, in addition to those*

*already employed, for the conversion
of the heathen, viz: the Christian
Colony; and that as the enterprise is
now, as we believe, both practicable
and desirable, this Convention will
adopt, at an early day, measures to
organize bodies of converted freedmen,
and aid them in settling as
missionary churches in Africa.*

This was not getting better, Greg thought.

*Some Southern Baptists,
after the Civil War, continued to
invoke the Curse of Ham theory while
others used the Mark of Cain premise
to justify the continued thought that the
Negro was meant to be a servant the
white race.*

*The Mark of Cain was
taken from the story of Cain who killed
his brother Abel in the Book of
Genesis.*

*In the King James Version
it reads, [15] And the LORD said unto
him, Therefore whosoever slayeth Cain,
vengeance shall be taken on him
sevenfold. And the LORD set a mark
upon Cain.*

*Some Southern Baptists,
and others along with them, believed*

this "mark" was a change in Cain's skin color from white to black. That thinking was then used to perpetuate an attitude that even extended to the Church.

I'm dead, Greg thought. *Even sweet Aunt Brenda is not going to go for any of this racial hatchet job.*

And instead of better it continued to get worse.

The number of lynchings were down.

What? Greg agonized. *You've got to be kidding me.*

Southern Baptist Convention

Resolution Concerning Lynching And Race Relations
Oklahoma City, Oklahoma - 1939.

1. That we record our gratitude that for the year 1938 the number of lynchings decreased and that only six lives were sacrificed to mob violence; That it brings a deep sense of sorrow and shame to us, both as citizens and Christians, that this form of lawlessness should still persist to any degree; That we pledge ourselves and urge all citizens to contend earnestly for the administration of justice under the orderly processes of law,

*reaffirming our unalterable opposition
to all forms of mob violence.*

*2. That while lynching is not due
wholly to racial antipathies nor the
victims of lynching limited to any one
race, it is beyond doubt or question
that racial antipathies are often one
of the chief contributing causes; That
we are glad to believe and have many
good reasons to believe that as
between the white and colored races
within the bounds of this Convention
racial animosities are growing less
and racial understanding and
cooperation are increasing, as
indicated by the fact that the white
people of the South, especially our
Baptist pastors and churches, are
establishing and maintaining
frequent contacts of a friendly and
helpful nature with the Negro race;
That we urge our Baptist people
everywhere to maintain and extend
these friendly and helpful contacts
and relations, remembering always
the law of Christian obligation that
the strong should bear the burdens of
the weak, and yet doing this without
any spirit of patronizing or air of
condescending.*

Greg turned forward a few more pages of

resolutions to 1961.

Resolution On Race Relations

St. Louis, Missouri - 1961

This Convention in years past has expressed itself clearly and positively on issues related to race relations. Today the solution of the race problem is a major challenge to Christian faith and action at home and abroad.

Because Southern Baptists are the largest Christian group in the area where racial tensions between whites and Negroes are most acute, we feel an especially keen sense of Christian responsibility in this hour.

We recognize that members of our churches have sincere differences of opinion as to the best course of action in this matter. On solid scriptural grounds, however, we reject mob violence as an attempted means of solving this problem. We believe that both lawless violence on one hand and unwarranted provocation on the other are outside the demands of Christ upon us all.

*We believe that the race problem is
a moral and spiritual as well as
social problem. Southern Baptists
accept the teachings of the Bible
and the Commission of Christ as
our sole guide of faith and practice
in this area as in every other area.
We cannot afford to let pride or
prejudice undermine . . . either our
Christian witness at home or the
years of consecrated, sacrificial
missionary service among all the
peoples of the world.*

*We therefore urge all Southern
Baptists to speak the truth of
Christ in love as it relates to all
those for whom he died. We further
urge that this Convention reaffirm
its conviction that every man has
dignity and worth before the Lord.
Let us commit ourselves as
Christians to do all that we can to
improve the relations among all
races as a positive demonstration of
the power of Christian love.*

Now we're getting somewhere, Greg thought.

This was seven years ago and a positive
positioning on Christian love is finally being spoken.
Greg would be able to tell Melinda, her family, and the
wonderful people at Trinity Street Baptist that he

helped this manuscript become a book because it showed the overcoming by the current Baptists and how they have evolved (*no can't use evolved*, Greg chided himself) into a contemporary force for justice and equally.

At the start of the next chapter Greg recognized the name Wallie Amos Criswell, W.A. Criswell. Every Baptist had heard of him. Greg knew Melinda's father was a big fan of the white-haired Patriarch of the Faith. He also knew that while Dr. Dothan and Dr. Criswell were church growth rivals, Dothan had mentioned Criswell from his own pulpit several of the Sundays that Greg was at Mountainview. And in one of those mentions Dothan reported that his good friend and popular evangelist Billy Graham was a member of Dr. Criswell's First Baptist Dallas Church. Chap's book had turned the corner. The second half will be a positive testimony to the redemptive work of Southern Baptists. Maybe he could somehow show only the second half of the book to Melinda's father.

Greg had never heard W. A. Criswell preach, but he had heard since he was a kid what a great, animated preacher he was. Now Chap was going to focus on one of the great man's sermons.

In February of 1956, Chap wrote. W.A. Criswell delivered a what came to be known as "The Fiery Sermon" to a group gathered for a Baptist evangelism conference in South Carolina.

> *First Baptist Church of*
> *Columbia hosted the overflow crowd there*

*to hear Criswell's booming voice exhort
fellow preachers to be true ministers of the
Gospel of Jesus Christ and that their
ministry will surely lead to a "baptism by
fire." As an example of their fiery ordeals
he referenced the attack of the forces of
desegregation.*

WHAT? Greg was not going to stop until this was over.

*Criswell shouted his disappointment at
the reluctance of ministers, "whose
forbearers and predecessors were martyrs
and were burned at the stake" but who
themselves refuse to speak up about
"this thing of integration."*

Greg laid the manuscript in his lap and rested his head forward on the seat in front of him. He broke his last promise to himself to not stop until it was complete. But this was too much for one sitting.

What am I going to do? He agonized. If he had not caught up with the bus and re-captured Chap's book, he would not be held to a promise whose object was lost. But he did recover it. He was going have to make this work somehow. He had faced a lot in his twenty-one years. Some words on paper were not going to defeat him… he hoped.

*Criswell went on to
denounce the Supreme Court for the
"foolishness" and "idiocy" of their*

ruling that he believed was meant to force integration onto the Christian South. "Let them integrate. Let them sit up there in their dirty shirts and make all their fine speeches. But they are all a bunch of infidels, dying from the neck up."

"True ministers," he said, must passionately resist government mandated desegregation because it is "a denial of all that we believe in," and to resist people and groups that were "two-by scathing, good-for-nothing fellows who are trying to upset all of the things that we love as good old Southern people and as good old Southern Baptists."

Greg put the book down. He would have to finish it another time.

Greg looked out at the passing parade of fences, rocks, and Burma Shave signs aglow in the setting sun and slowly nodded off.

"Medic! Medic! Get over here!" the Major shouted.

Greg slid along the wet earth, dragging his bag. His NCO had scratched off the Red Cross on his helmet before he left camp.

"Gooks think it's funny to aim at these. There. Now you may make it a week or two."

The humor turned dark the moment Greg got to his duty station. When death is the punch line there is no reason for the set-up to be subtle.

Once Greg reached the wounded soldier, the Major grabbed Greg's right hand and shoved it up to his wrist into the wounded boy's abdomen.

"Feel the bleeder?"

"I think so."

"Then stop it and keep it stopped 'til someone gets here with a stretcher." The Major stood and started yelling obscenity-laced commands at kids too young to get into a Grateful Dead concert.

With his fist again up to his watch in a Marine, Greg thought to himself, "I'm not supposed to be here."

"Sergeant, Sergeant," the bus driver shook Greg's shoulder. "This is Las Cruces."

Instinctively Greg checked his hands for blood and then thanked the bus driver as he came back to New Mexico and reality.

Greg stayed awake the rest of the trip. He didn't need another unconscious trip to the Delta. Every part of his life was now in front of him, Interstate10 all the way to Houston.

The bus driver stood and said in a loud voice, "This is Seguin, folks. This will be our last stop before Houston. You might want to get a bite here and not pay those Houston prices."

Greg thought he would just stay on the bus. But he had enough money for a sandwich. The "Mayor's Special" had worn off and the bus was still three hours from Houston. All of his fellow travelers were already inside Kirby's Korner Kactice Kafe before he walked in the door. There was one empty table, but it was a table for six.

"Sit anywhere," a large Mexican woman directed.

"This okay?" Greg asked pointing to the sizable table.

The large woman was not happy about it, but shrugged. Greg sat at one end and placed Chap's book on the plate to his left. A thinner young waitress death spiraled with the larger one like Olympic skating pairs. The thinner did not impress the local judges by making her moves holding a pitcher of iced tea, two glasses of water, and a stack of menus under her right armpit, but Greg was. She slammed the water glasses down in front of two older regulars wearing straw cowboy hats, and refilled three iced tea glasses with the same arm that clamped the menus. She zoomed past Greg but managed to deal him an uncomfortably warm menu on her way by.

"Tea or coffee?"

"Iced tea."

"Someone joining you?" she asked, looking at the manuscript in the plate next to Greg.

"Nope. Just me."

"Well, all right then," Thinner said as she drew her order pad out of her apron belt like Marshall Dillon drawing his single-action Colt. Then, just as fast she pulled a yellow pencil from behind her left ear.

"Know what you want, Handsome? I'm on the right there, under desserts."

"Not yet."

"I'll be back."

The large woman and the thinner performed an encore in the opposite direction and still did not spill a drop of tea or slab of pie. The moves affirmed they were returning champions of the greasy-joint Olympics.

Greg scanned the walls of the friendly place and among fading photos and deer heads was a sign that read, "Best Hamburger in Seguin." Under the sign were small banners for 1964, 1966, and 1967. Greg was glad he did not pass through in 1965.

Thinner was back. "How about it, Handsome?"

"I'll try a hamburger."

"All the way?"

"Sure. Wait, no onions."

"Got a date? I like a man that smells like raaaww onions."

Thinner quit trying. Greg rested his gym bag on top of the table to hold his place but also where he could watch it. He crossed the crowded room to the payphone next to the short hall that led to the restrooms. He put a dime in the slot and dialed Aunt Brenda's still long distance number. He watched his gym bag as he heard his dime drop into the metal scoop near the bottom of the Southwestern Bell wall hanging. When the operator came on the line Greg said, "Collect call from Greg, please ma'am." Aunt Brenda's phone started to ring. It rang six times. She did not pick up.

"Sorry," the operator said, "please try again later."

Greg saw his burger next to his gym bag as he hung up. He had tried to call her from Kingman, Arizona and got no answer then as well. He was calling to ask her to pick him up from the bus station but now, having called twice with no answer, Greg was starting to get concerned. Greg didn't have enough cash to take a cab all the way to Aunt Brenda's but he was sure he could make it with one more bus trip. This time it would be local.

Greg left half the tip he would have because he was afraid he would need his extra change for the local bus in Houston, if his Aunt Brenda did not pick him up.

Greg sipped iced tea and thought about calling Melinda. It was getting late and he didn't want to call her "collect". Just before the bus pulled away from the last greasy diner of the trip, Greg stared out his window at still-dancing Thinner inside and thought about how long it had been since he had worried about onions on burgers.

Greg chewed his last stick of Juicy Fruit until all the juicy and most of the fruit was gone. He suddenly wanted to spit the gum out.

Greg unzipped his gym bag and found the bus schedule he had picked up on his departure way back in California. The no longer needed souvenir schedule was the perfect place for a small wad of gum. Greg spit his used rubbery glob onto the schedule, wrapped it, put it in a side zippered pocket, and repositioned Chap's manuscript on a bed of whites and shaving supplies. With all preparations ready for arrival, Greg leaned back in his now-familiar seat cushion with almost an hour to think about the old days in Houston one more time.

CHAPTER 9

Reagan High School

Houston

March 7, 1964

Melinda Cook was a beauty, and smart. Never-made-a-B smart. Greg was nominated for "most handsome" a couple of years, but never won. Greg was smarter than he let people, especially teachers, know. Being tagged "a brain" could get a guy hurt between classes at his middle class high school. No one was "a brain" and "cool." "Cool" was the ultimate brand goal of pre- and post-pubescent boys. "Jock" was pretty cool, but "Cool" was cooler. Greg was not leather jacket, longhaired, "hood" cool, the edgiest and highest form of cool left over from the 50's. Greg was clean-cut, wheat jean, madras and Ban Lon wearing "parent cool." "Parent cool" was unquestionably down the cool scale from "Jock" and slightly above the often horned-rimmed-glasses-wearing, uncool "brain" type. But Greg was well liked and even with the huge Baby-Boomer class sizes, Greg was at least Wally-brother-of-the-Beave popular.

Greg was a junior when Melinda was a sophomore. Melinda thought they made a good-looking couple. Greg thought she was Christian "hot." At Reagan some girls wore mini-skirts and were constantly engaging with the hem-length police. While Melinda showed a lot of great leg, she was never yardstick challenged.   Greg started going to Melinda's huge church shortly after their second date. Greg's Mom and Jack were not happy.

It was softball season and Melinda's church's 18 and under team had gone to State two years in a row. Greg loved softball, and his church, Jack's church, only had a men's team and half of the men on it did not even actually attend Trinity Street. In fact, the third baseman and catcher were both Catholic.

Greg was a natural at second. Melinda's church, Mountainview Baptist, had a star second baseman last season, but he had turned 18 and joined the Army before the current season started.

In Greg's view, Mountainview had several odd things about it.

First, there were no mountains in Houston. And second was the pastor, Dr. T. Wallace Dothan. Greg had heard of him all of his life. He had pastored Mountainview since 1945. He was the only pastor Greg ever knew who did not call himself reverend or pastor. Melinda confided in Greg that she heard some women in the restroom talking one time about his title. It seemed that "Dr." came from an honorary degree some West Virginia college gave him for raising money to build a gym.

But he looked every inch the part of a Baptist preacher. From his expensive toupee down to his white patent leather Stacy Adams. His bought hair <u>was</u> longer than the hairstyles of many of his crew cut or neatly trimmed deacons. It was never hippie-length but his expensive rug let everyone know he kept up with what was "happenin'" even if he wasn't happenin' himself. Two of the many things Dothan did not abide were Catholics and long-haired Hippies.

"Does he think that thing is fooling anybody?" Greg asked Melinda.

"Shh," Melinda said joining in the Great Fake Rug Conspiracy of 1965.

One thing about Dr. Dothan was true. The man could preach. Anytime he stepped into the huge white Mountainview pulpit his voice filled every nook of the enormous sanctuary. From that raised platform he did have a Mountain View. Dr. Dothan's booming voice roared from the mountain and then could be dialed down to syrupy sweet and back up to thunder-power in the blink of a verse. He quite literally scared the hell out of many of his converts.

The pastor may have been an honorary doctor but he bled Baptist. His powerful voice thundered, not only through the thousand seats at Mountainview, but across the Southern Baptist Convention. When teams at the Nashville headquarters wanted to know what they really thought about a particularly troubling subject, they would telegraph Dr. T. Wallace Dothan and he would tell them.

The third odd thing was that Dothan did not scare Greg. At Trinity Street Baptist Greg had gotten a surprisingly strong foundation in the Word of God. Greg believed that God was the one in power and with that power mixed with love, God sent his son Jesus to save us. That was real power and no Kentucky Fried Chicken-looking fake colonel was going to scare Greg. What did bother Greg was the power Dr. Dothan had over Melinda's father and their family.

Melinda's father was one of those neatly trimmed deacons that did Dothan's bidding with a sense of pride and confidence. And like Dr. Dothan, Melinda's father bled Baptist. His family had been Baptists all the way back to its beginnings. Melinda's great, great something had been a part of the Great Awakening and the establishment of Baptist churches across the South.

Unlike the fake-haired pastor, Melinda's father did scare Greg. He was the one in Greg's life that held the power over what Greg wanted more than anything, Melinda. Melinda adored her father and would never say or do anything against his wishes. Melinda's father was not fond of the fact that they were not dating other people. He did not believe that Greg was "the one" for his daughter but he cared enough for her and his own home environment to keep it pleasant and only undermine Melinda's feelings about Greg in the subtlest of ways. Even with Melinda's love for her father she also loved Greg. This caused pressures within her and her choices that Greg never realized.

During a make-out session, if things were getting a little too steamy, Melinda would come up for air with, "Did you know my father was a marksman in the Boy Scouts?"

The sudden *What?* in Greg's mind had the exact effect Melinda intended. Three mood-killers in one short question. Her father, a rifle, and Boy Scouts. Greg had only gone as far as Webelos after Cub Scouts. Greg was much more interested in sports than rubbing sticks and helping little old ladies. But by high school it was one of those decisions that added to the many that could bring on guilt at any moment.

As Melinda and Greg got more serious and their make-out sessions got more frequent, and not always initiated by Greg, he learned more about Melinda's father than he knew about President Kennedy and Greg knew a lot about President Kennedy.

He learned her father had a sister who died tragically as a child at a railroad crossing. He played tailback in college until his knee was wrecked on a dirty play. He voted for FDR but hated most Democrats. He met Melinda's mother at a neighborhood park square dance and that was the last time they danced together. And the only time she ever saw him cry was when Old Yeller died.

Melinda never shared information about her mother the same way. Greg had seen a picture of Melinda's mother when she was in high school. She was almost as pretty as Melinda. They looked very much alike. Greg would stare at her briefly sometimes and think that was how Melinda would look when she got to her age, whatever ancient number that was. But looking at her mother, he was good with that.

No relation to her looks, Melinda's mother was a terrible cook. Greg's mother cooked what he thought everyone did; cheap steak beaten to a pulp and fried in a skillet, served alongside mashed potatoes, little green peas from a can, with vanilla Mellorine and Hershey's syrup for dessert.

Unlike Greg's Mother, Melinda's mother fixed fancy vegetables from a pressure cooker, baked fish from a cookbook, and ended with cottage cheese and peaches without the syrup you could drink from the can. It was no wonder to Greg how much Melinda enjoyed a Prince's cheeseburger and onion rings. Greg did not know if Melinda's mother was as Baptist as Melinda's father but Greg never went to Mountainview when Melinda's mother was not there with Melinda and her father.

Chap's book was going to kill her parents and probably any chance he still had with Melinda.

The two things that drew Greg to Mountainview Baptist were Melinda and softball. Greg really wanted to play ball and since he wasn't going to play the next year in college this would be his last season.

When Greg told his Mom and Jack about "attending" Mountainview, they were not pleased. But

Jack had played ball and it had meant a lot to him. If
Trinity Street had enough boys for a team, Jack would
have coached and that would have been that. But a
Trinity Street team was not going to happen that year.
So, if not happy, they were pleased that at least it was a
Baptist church and not some cult like the
Episcopalians.

Jack the Baptist secretly was torn about
Mountainview. He hated the fact that large churches
they were starting to call mega-churches were crippling
small congregations like Trinity Street. Jack felt the
smaller churches served their neighborhoods, neighbors
and members better than the cavernous cathedrals of
churches like Mountainview. But Jack was enough of a
realist to understand that teens, and often their parents,
were attracted to the programs and amenities that only
the larger churches could afford to offer. But the
oddest thing was that Jack liked Dothan. Jack had
maybe known him in an earlier time.

The charismatic, in the sense of his ability to
attract people to the church not the Pentecostal sense,
Dr. Dothan brought them in from all over. His new
television show, "Just What the Doctor Ordered with
Dr. T. Wallace Dothan" was a kind of a Christian
Johnny Carson Show. His colorful, talented choir
director became "Minstrel Mark" the leader of the band
and the Mountainview Mountaintop Singers and was
the foil for much of the trying-too-hard TV Pastor's
demeaning humor. The Doctor was no Johnny Carson
or Billy Graham but the show was very popular and
during Greg's short time at Mountainview, Sunday

morning worship attendance almost doubled to nearly 5,000. Much of this was connected to the TV show.

The Mountainview softball coach required, and Melinda coaxed, Greg to attend Sunday services every week. The young couple would sit in the back out of sight of Melinda's parents, except when her Father took up the collection. Greg would look up hymn titles that he thought were funny and try to crack Melinda up during even the most serious parts of the sermon. But between the kidding around and trying to rub her knee with his, Greg did hear things. While the Good Doctor was not Greg's favorite person, the words of God's writing did thunder out of his mouth and a few landed in that place in his heart right next to where he kept Melinda. Greg had heard much the same word from quieter, less handkerchief-brow-mopping preachers than Dothan, but his words did matter.

The Fourth of July was also Founder's Day at Mountainview Baptist. This year July 4th was on a Saturday. Every year the members and former members of Mountainview had a huge picnic under the Founder's Tree.

The Founder's Tree was an old southern live oak that stretched out 80 feet across. The bark of the old tree was dark and rigid and scaled like an armadillo designed by Picasso. A 12-inch brass plaque had been a part of the historic oak for so many years, it now

looked embossed in the tree. The plaque told the story
of the twelve founders of Mountainview Baptist that
first met under it. Here on that rise, certainly not
worthy of a Mountainview, twelve believers came
together to commit to building a church that would last
as long and grow as large as that mighty oak.

Greg had always spent the Fourth of July with
his Mother and Jack in New Braunfels. Greg loved
New Braunfels. He loved the cool Comal River that
meandered at the perfect speed for an inner tube and a
tan, the public golf course where he learned to play, the
taste of his first *Big Red* in a tall paper cup at the little
hut at the end of the first nine, and going back to the
tourist court swimming pool where older teenage girls
wore two piece swim suits and sometimes smiled at
him.

And the fireworks on Fourth. Jack would lie on
the same green he had three-putted hours earlier in the
day and watch a dark New Braunfels sky light up
brighter than Walt Disney's Wonderful World of Color
on their new color TV. The evening ended with
authentic strudel for dessert at Schultz's, watching an
old German guy stare at his thick clear glass goblet of
beer like a fortuneteller gazing into her crystal orb. It
was a place of wonderful memories.

Greg would have loved to have taken Melinda
to New Braunfels just to have sat holding hands on the
number eight green and watch the sky fill with magical
lights. But Greg had commitments to honor, both to
the team playing an 11a.m. game in the searing
Houston heat that morning and to the Founder's

Fourth celebration at Mountainview. That Saturday Greg was missing the strudel, the cool Comal River that kept so many of the driving range balls he played with, his mother and even Jack. Melinda's family was nice enough to him but it was never the same.

Jack and Greg's mother said they understood when they drove off. Greg knew they knew this was really about Melinda and not a commitment to his teammates. And it was certainly not about Founder's Day and a toupee wearing Baptist in a Hawaiian shirt under an old tree. Greg hoped they would miss him at the bakery and at Ol' Bossy when they got their cones. There were things Greg liked about getting older, but sipping lemonade from a powdered mix was nowhere close to a Big Red at the turn.

Just then, a shapely vision silhouetted by the setting sun made growing up not nearly as bad as he was feeling. Melinda took Greg's hand and pulled him to his feet. Greg tossed the rest of his cup of powdered-mix lemonade in a trashcan and they left the shadow of the Founder's Tree for the sunshine and fun.

"Don't go too far," Melinda's mother warned. That was the last thing Greg wanted Melinda to hear.

Trinity Street Baptist Church

Thursday July 23, 1964

Trinity Street was having a Youth Revival. The Beatles' first movie, "A Hard Day's Night" had just had its American premiere. Some longhaired, Beatle-cut seminary hothead was going to small churches and optimistically holding summer night services for large groups of Baby Boomers. One of these rockin' roadshows even had drums. The depression-era Baptists of Trinity Street imagined this blasphemy horrifically leading to only one tragic outcome... dancing.

Wednesdays, even when on a school night, were okay for church for many. From Sunbeams to Royal Ambassadors, Girls Auxiliary and beyond filled the evening for the youth while the adults had yet another service. Greg's parents were not Wednesday kind of Baptists, even in the summer.

Summer or not, for Melinda's parents, church anywhere but Mountainview was not something up for consideration. Sneaking off to park was one thing for Greg and Melinda, but sneaking off to church, even to a youth revival, seemed weirdly wrong. So, Melinda sweet-talked her father and he folded like a whitened dress shirt on a Tide commercial.

Of course, Jack and Greg's Mom were delighted Greg was coming back to Trinity Street, Thursday night or not. Jack barbequed for Melinda and Greg before going to church that evening. Jack really wanted to go along but Greg's Mom convinced him to stay home with her and watch *The Munsters* and *Gilligan's Island*. Jack reluctantly agreed and even gave Greg the keys to his Lincoln. Jack and Greg's Mom both liked Melinda very much. They had never met Melinda's family. Greg thought maybe sometime at a Mountainview ballgame the four would meet. *Or at the wedding* he laughed to himself.

Greg parked Jack's Lincoln under a street lamp out front instead of the dark parking lot behind the church. Some neighborhood kids would cut through that parking lot and chunk rocks at the lights on the poles. Greg never admitted to having developed his throwing arm back there but he never denied it either.

Once they walked up the front steps they could hear the music. This was no droning hymns from the Civil War, this was real music. Up-tempo guitar music with a strange-looking keyboard that made stranger but very cool sounds replaced the traditional organ music. Greg nodded to a couple of friends, but since the music had already started Melinda and Greg took a seat on the first empty long wooden pew. Familiar songs with new arrangements, new songs with strange lyrics and beats, it was all very different from what both were used to but they got into it very fast. And then a couple of rows up, several girls started doing something Greg had never seen in church. They started clapping with the music. Soon everyone, including Melinda, was clapping. Greg was the last to join the informal percussionists, but soon did and liked it as much as anyone.

And then the young evangelist got up and moved to the pulpit. He thanked the band and told a very hip Christian joke. He got everybody to move up to fill all the pews up front. He shook his long hair that actually covered the top of his ears. His sideburns were

114

growing in longer than anyone's at high school.

Being back in those wooden pews at Trinity Street, Greg remembered.

When Greg was eleven he left the money counters, Jack and chocolate milk get-a-ways and returned to the sanctuary to sit with his friends. Greg knew that even though he was sitting with four Dennis the Menaces, his Mother was pleased to have him back in the sanctuary.

One Sunday Greg felt all the teaching and reading and hearing about Jesus and his love come alive within him. Jesus was there. Greg and God made a secret pact that morning. But through a thousand choruses of *Just As I Am* and *I Surrender All*, Greg never let go of the back of the pew in front of him to walk down the aisle to make what the Baptist preachers called a "public profession of faith."

As Greg got older everyone just assumed he had. Both his Mother and Jack the Baptist had talked with him about it and knew about his eleven-year-old secret decision.

Melinda and Greg talked about everything from music, to Jesus to making out. But Melinda was one of the many who just assumed.

But that night amongst the music and stories of forgiveness, Jesus came back. As everyone stood for the up-tempo version of *Amazing Grace,* Greg took his familiar grip on the rounded pew back in front of him. Greg loved to hear Melinda sing but that night with her lips only inches from his ear all he could hear was "the call."

If he did this, Melinda might feel like he had kept this from her. If he did this everyone would be staring at him. If he did this… Greg let go of the pew and stepped into the aisle. The old red aisle carpet seemed to rise behind him creating a wave on which he surfed to the front where Beatle-cut smiled and held out an open welcoming hand. Greg had done it.

"What did your Mom say?" Melinda whispered to Greg on the upstairs phone outside her room.

"She and Jack congratulated me like I'd won the batting title or something," Greg said from the phone near the kitchen at his house.

"It's late Greggy," his mom shouted from her room.

"I'm so proud of you," Melinda continued. "Being in heaven without you would be awful. Although nothing's awful in heaven but you know what I mean."

He knew what she meant. She loved him. That was better than winning the batting title or a golden glove.

"What did your father say?" Greg asked.

"Well…he said if he had known you weren't saved he would have never let you date me. Ooh! Got to go," as she hung up.

Founder's Day Fourth always ended with all the Mountainview choirs getting together and singing "Hymns Through the Ages" followed by a short, for him, sermon from the Hawaiian-shirted Dr. Dothan.

Somewhere between "The Old Rugged Cross" and "I'll Fly Away" a police car pulled up. Greg told Melinda that Dothan was probably being busted by the bad-hairpiece police. But then Greg saw that his Aunt Brenda was with them. Greg's Aunt Brenda was a zinnia-growing, Betty Crocker-baking, quiet person who was nothing like her out-going sister, Greg's mother.

The policeman and Aunt Brenda spotted Greg and walked toward him. Greg could tell his Aunt Brenda had been crying. Greg knew something was very wrong.

The double funeral was, of course, at Trinity Street Baptist. Greg sat in a dark suit Jack had bought him months earlier. Aunt Brenda cried on his right and Melinda cried on his left. Nice things were probably said. Greg was surprised to see Dr. Dothan there. He sat with Melinda's parents who were nice enough to come and bring someone important instead of flowers. Greg sat there. No tears, no fears. He stared at the stained glass image of Jesus. Jesus was smiling. Greg was not. The old wooden pew he had left to give his life to Jesus not so long before was like his youth, far behind him.

      Greg's senior year he lived with his Aunt Brenda. She was single and the death of her only sister hit her hard. She needed "Greggy" that year as much as he needed a place to live.

      Aunt Brenda knew nothing about teenage boys or how they lived. She was shocked at Greggy's room the first and last time she went in there. She never complained and encouraged Greg to do his own thing. They had been through enough.

      With the tragedy still bumper-riding close in the rear view mirror of his inherited Lincoln, Greg determined to make the best of his senior year. Greg had been accepted to Baylor like his parents had wanted, and the insurance would easily pay for tuition and Penland Hall where he would be staying. So all the worrying about "what's next" was settled for a while. Melinda would join Greg at Baylor when she graduated the next year and then, without the specter of Dr. Dothan and Melinda's father, they would relax and just be the couple they had always wanted to be.

The couple in the front seat they were "doubling" with had gotten very quiet. Every time Greg had suggested they check out the imaginary submarine races at the reflection pond at Hermann Park, Melinda had said no. This time his friend Tommy was driving and Greg and Melinda did not have a choice. When the front seat went to park, the back seat went along.

God bless Tommy, Greg thought.

Now, while Melinda was certainly a "good girl," she and Greg did their share of "parking" and "making out." Melinda loved the way Greg held her face in his hands the first time he kissed her. His hands were strong and gentle at the same time. However, Melinda had been taught by her friend, Diane, that she could not get carried away in the moment. Melinda knew it was up to her not to let Greg get too "worked up." A lot of her after-movie choices depended on the movie they had just watched.

If they went to the Majestic Theater to see a comedy or Western a little parking was okay with her. But, if they saw something testosterone-raising like

"Goldfinger", Melinda would step out under the marquee lights and have a sudden craving for a pineapple Dr. Pepper from the Pig Stand drive-in on North Shepherd. By the time Greg walked her to the door, he had almost forgotten Pussy Galore. Almost. Greg did remember that Melinda's father was always just on the other side of the lighted doorstep.

Greg's Senior Prom was a blast. The band was really good. They could jump from Sam the Sham and the Pharaohs' "Wooly Bully" to The Righteous Brothers' "You've Lost That Lovin' Feelin'" in a heartbeat. It was a time when everybody talked about spiking the punch and sneaking into bars after the dance, but no one that Greg or Melinda knew actually did. Greg and Melinda sat with friends and laughed at and with many of the seniors in Greg's class. A couple of Melinda's friends, who were also dating seniors, took Melinda off to spend some time together. This gave Greg and Tommy a chance to goof on more seniors and check out "babes" for Tommy. Greg didn't tell anyone, even Tommy, that he and Melinda were going to an after prom party the church was having. Graduating senior or not, that news could damage even his "parent cool" image.

He wasn't going because Melinda insisted. In fact, he flattered himself into thinking she would probably go anywhere he wanted. But by this time, he found he enjoyed making Melinda happy.

Tommy and Greg hit the buffet and loaded up a couple of plates for the table. Greg, Tommy, Melinda, and Tommy's date all got back to the table at the same time. Melinda was great. Then suddenly the band played "their song."

Dang, Greg thought.

During one especially active make-out session in Greg's car, Melinda halted everything with, "What about dancing?" Greg's first thought was, *"Here? It's cold outside."* But at that point Melinda continued.

"I hear the band is going to be great."

Greg realized she was talking about the Prom. After he had reserved a tux and Melinda had made her own dress and a pocket-handkerchief, cummerbund, and bow tie from the same material for him, Greg put the Prom out of his mind. Especially at that moment. But dancing?

Greg's Mom, without Jack's knowledge, taught Greg to dance the summer he was twelve. Before Jack the non-dancing Baptist, Greg's Mom had loved to dance. She dated dapper young men who would take her to dances. Greg did not like his Mother leaving but he did like seeing her in her beautiful dance gowns. As she taught Greggy the simple dance steps to old Russ Morgan music, Greg could tell he wasn't too bad at it.

But like intelligence, he didn't want anyone to know. The reasoning was simple. The culture of cool demands that one is in control of all body parts at all times and any movement of a part, without the utmost necessity, can kill the "cool." Dancing, especially fast dancing, required rapid body part movements and if you weren't certain American Bandstand regulars, the action would break every rule of cool.

Another great thing about Melinda was that she was Baptist and everybody knew "Baptists don't dance." So when she suddenly brought up the subject, Greg was thrown off his game.

"Dance? Do you dance?" Greg asked.

"I love to dance."

"But we're Baptist."

"True, but-"

"Well, maybe," Greg said. "But I'm really not much of a dancer."

"Me neither, but we just can't go to your Prom and not dance one dance, can we?"

Greg smiled a crooked smile and tried to remember if he had ever explained "cool" to her.

But that night at the Prom, Greg was putty in her white elbow length gloved hands.

Melinda and Greg tried to synchronize their moves in the darkened room with the star-like reflections of the mirror ball dancing better than they were. Greg was wishing "our song" had been a little less up-tempo, but they both loved the Beatles and "I Saw Her Standing There" was the perfect song for "their song."

Twenty-two months earlier, Greg and Tommy were walking down the locker-lined hallway near the gym when Greg noticed Melinda for the first time. She was alone, clutching more books to her chest than Greg had read in his entire educational life. She had a faraway look as students floated by like brook trout. Greg, with more nerve and less cool than ever, started singing the popular Beatles song, "I Saw Her Standing There." Greg was never sure if it was his singing voice or attention that made her smile and not hit him with her *War and Peace* hard back. Tommy tried his best Liverpool accent, which wouldn't have fooled Helen Keller. But two weeks later Greg, without Tommy, and Melinda were at a football game and twenty-two months later they were dancing to "our song."

The music thankfully shifted to the slower "Mr. Tambourine Man." Greg held her right hand in his left as his right hand slipped around her prom-dressed waist. Soon she released his right hand and put her arms around his neck. He put both arms around her waist as she rested her French Twist on his strong right shoulder. The two transcended the swaying brook trout around them and they floated to a place of quiet contentment. Greg wondered why they hadn't done this before and Melinda wondered how Baptists could be against something so sweet and innocent. As the song transitioned to the beautiful "Stranger on the Shore," Melinda thought about the disciples seeing the stranger on the shore. It was a night of mixed images and magical music.

Suddenly, the overhead lights brightened a bit and the band starting whaling "Wooly Bully." Greg and Melinda separated and tried to keep up and then both started to laugh. Tommy "danced" over like an explorer in snowshoes crossing the La Brea Tar Pits. Greg and Tommy started dueting the meaningful lyrical advice to "Get you someone really to pull the wool with you. Wooly bully, wooly bully."

The three were convulsing with laughter. Tommy's date didn't get it.

Greg loved Melinda's laugh.

CHAPTER 10

Baylor University, Waco, Texas

September 1965

Penland Hall was a great dorm. Modern enough that it stuck out on an historic campus with an 1845 start. Beautiful old trees lined paths leading to grand, stately buildings that felt as old as the trees. Greg's freshman roommates were eclectic and great. One was an affable Yankee with a Mormon girlfriend at Brigham Young. The other was a Texas boy who was very much smarter than he looked except when he was talking in his sleep. Each student had a small desk with a corkboard over it. The Yankee took the lower bunk and the sleep-talker took the upper. Greg had the single twin bed on the other side of the room, which in this case was about six feet away. On their personal bulletin board, each roommate thumbtacked a picture of his girlfriend back home. Melinda was by far the prettiest.

Classes for Greg did not match the beauty of the campus. Class after class Greg realized that the other students had been better prepared, or actually paid attention to get their grades good enough, to get into Baylor. Greg had not. Entrance tests and former easily won grades were history the minute Greg stepped into History 101 and all of his other classes. Within a few short weeks on campus, Greg went from a happy, carefree kid with a beautiful steady girlfriend, to an unhappy, aging teenager.

Away from home, the sudden emptiness of losing his Mom at such a critical time in his life overcame him. Things he had said and "thank you's" he had not said to Jack kept him awake in his twin bed six feet away from the night-mumbling stranger and the Mormon-loving Yankee.

That first semester at Baylor Greg felt three things he could never remember feeling before: alone, depressed, and stupid. Over semester break, instead of going home to Houston, Greg got food poisoning. He threw-up in his sink because he couldn't make it to the toilets down the hall. He was glad his roommates missed that but he had never felt so alone and miserable. A note was slid under his door. The notice of his academic probation for his second semester had mistakenly been delivered to another student.

One by one dorm mates throughout Penland took down their high school sweethearts' pictures off the corkboards. A couple of months into classes, one good-looking, smart young man made it out to the new Lake Waco and killed himself because he worried his grades, falling below A's, would disappoint his now-grieving parents. In the weird thoughts that ran through Greg's head at a time like that, was the one that he was glad he didn't have parents that put that kind of pressure on him.

Baylor had come off years of great football teams led by All American Don Trull. Trull had won the Sammy Baugh award for the nation's best passer twice and in 1963 he finished fourth for the Heisman. Jack got tickets for himself and Greg to the 1963 Bluebonnet Bowl in Houston. Trull and the Baylor Bears were matched against an always tough LSU team. Trull was named most valuable player in Baylor's 14-7 victory. The thought of Greg going to that same school made Jack very proud.

But now Jack was gone, Trull was quarterbacking the Houston Oilers, and Greg and the Baylor Bears struggled. Unlike Greg that season, the Bears managed to break even.

Freshmen could not have cars at Baylor. Greg sold Jack's Lincoln and used the money for his food plan and other necessities. Aunt Brenda had access to his insurance money and would send Greg cash when he asked for it.

Without a car, going back to Houston, even in his second semester wasn't easy. He rode the bus home once. It was a terrible experience. Greg vowed to never ride a bus again. Melinda and her parents came up one weekend for a game and for her to familiarize herself with the campus. The discomfort of being with her parents as they launched what seemed like thousands of questions at him, many of which could have been answered by showing the three of them the letter of academic probation, made Melinda's visit less than grand. She could tell he had changed. He could tell she knew he was changing.

Going back for her prom had none of the laughter and fun of his. Tommy wasn't there and neither was their teenage infatuation. He thought about lying to her and telling her he had taken her picture off his corkboard like so many of the others in his dorm. Breaking up with the loser he was turning out to be would be best for Melinda.

He thought of it until he saw her in that dress. One thing about Greg had not changed. He was still infatuated with Melinda.

For the first time when they danced, Greg did not breathe in deeply to smell the mixture of her. Instead he noticed other senior boys and even a young teacher looking at Melinda. With his insecurity at an all-time low, Greg's vulnerability turned to jealousy. Melinda could tell he was mad. She saw the entire evening as unfair. She had done everything he wanted at his prom and would have done more. Greg was not even trying to make hers special.

In her car Melinda decided they needed to talk. There would be no submarine races at the park, no summer moistness of young love in Houston heat, no giggling at other's earlier antics and shortcomings, this was serious. Melinda was going to tell Greg how hurt she was by his behavior at her prom, how he need not try to make her graduation if he was going to act this way, and how she expected to be treated as his girlfriend when she got to Baylor. But Melinda did not get a chance to say any of that.

Going back for her prom had none of the
laughter and fun of his. Tommy wasn't there and
neither was their teenage infatuation. He thought about
lying to her and telling her he had taken her picture off
his corkboard like so many of the others in his dorm.
Breaking up with the loser he was turning out to be
would be best for Melinda.

128

Greg preemptively struck. He handed her a folded paper as he drove her car. She opened it but could not make out much of what it said under the light and dark moments created by the passing street lamps. Greg stopped at a red light and Melinda was able to read, "Enlistment Orders."

"What does this mean?" Melinda asked.

"Just what it says. I'm enlisting in the Air Force."

"Why?"

Greg thought of heroic answers about defending his country, defeating the Commie bastards, making Democracy free for all. But all he could come up with was, "I have to."

He told Melinda the truth about being on academic probation, about dropping a class he was failing, and about a second letter shoved under his door. The letter had said that because he was no longer taking a full load at college he was now eligible for the draft.

"The draft would mean Army," Greg said. What he didn't say was, the Army would mean Vietnam, and Vietnam would mean death for someone in Greg's already depressed state.

He told her with as bright a face as he could muster, how he visited recruiters and chose the Air Force. Great benefits including free college when he got out. Only four years of active duty.

"Four years!" Melinda screamed.

"Did I mention that is four years without anyone shooting at you? You'll be at Baylor that long. I will be back for your graduation and we can start a real adult life together."

"Will you leave this summer?" Melinda asked.

"Well, I passed my physical yesterday."

"Yesterday!"

"They gave me a week to get my things together. Too bad I don't have a week's worth of things to get together. I report to the downtown Post Office to leave from there Thursday morning."

"Thursday's not a week."

"Well, they gave me a week last Thursday."

Melinda's shock turned to sadness. She forgot all the points of her "talk."

Her left temple melted into Greg's right shoulder as he drove. Several tears took turns running down her cheek like the rollercoaster they rode at Stewart beach last summer.

Melinda reached up and turned on her radio. The first song on was "Chapel of Love." Melinda wondered if they would ever be going to the chapel. Greg pulled into the Pig Stand and ordered two pineapple Dr. Peppers from Jan the carhop. Melinda leaned even more into his shoulder, closed her eyes and listened to the music. A few more tears fell on the bodice of the prom dress she had worked so hard to make.

CHAPTER 11

20 miles from Houston

Thursday April 4, 1968

A young Black man moved to the music from a transistor radio held tight to his ear since he boarded in Seguin.

With Greg not being at Baylor, another losing season looming, and her father on the board of the infant Houston Baptist University, Melinda decided to stay home and attend HBU. It was the only alternative to Baylor that her parents saw as worthy. She was now a Dean's list sophomore and on her way to becoming some kind of teacher.

Melinda had received the new HBU scholarship from Mountainview Baptist and had to "volunteer" in the church office as part of the scholarship requirements. Greg had kept up with her through letters that he was not as good at returning as receiving. Her words were always loving and kind. Letter by letter her teenage angst and excitement matured into the writings of an experienced young woman filled with ideas for change and contemporary positions on public debates.. Her pro and anti stances included being pro-military but anti-war, pro-women's lib but anti-abortion, and pro-Democrat but anti-Johnson. She was also anti-death penalty, women preachers, and for some reason Bobby Goldsboro. Melinda never burned her bra but she did bake it at 325 degrees for 20 minutes one wintery Houston day.

Greg had no idea who he would be returning to, or frankly if she had only been nice to write encouragement to a high school boyfriend/Air Force guy in harm's way and would not even be home when he called. Greg checked his watch and ran it forward to 7:45pm Central Standard Time. The bus should arrive in Houston in less than-

"NO!" the young Black man roared. Everyone on the bus, including the driver, jumped. Before anyone could ask what happened he screamed, "They've KILLED HIM!"

"Who?" a near-by passenger asked.

But the young man started crying and quieted to, "They killed him. They killed him." The driver took an unscheduled exit at Sealy, stopped the bus and walked down the aisle to the inconsolable young man. The young man was able to give the bus driver a name.

"Martin Luther King."

Each passenger had a different reaction and a different question. The driver climbed back in his seat and got back on the highway to Houston.

Every image in Greg's mind was of Chap. Shot, dying and screaming, "MY BOOK! THEY HAVE TO SEE MY BOOK! THEY HAVE TO SEE-"

One of the passengers asked the young man if he could try to get something on his radio. The defeated man, who looked older than when he boarded the bus, weakly offered his precious possession to the fellow traveler. Without his radio and hope, the young man stared out into the darkness of that night. As the stranger's index finger rolled the slotted dialing wheel of the small radio up and down, Greg could occasionally hear a garbled broadcast amongst the static but nothing intelligible.

Over the next forty-five minutes the passenger would occasionally give the entire bus an update but nothing of any real new news.

Only a mile or two out, the passenger with the radio returned it to the young devastated man still holding the separated ear cord in his hand. Greg saw the Houston skyline come into view on his side of the bus. He had always liked downtown Houston and its skyline. It had been fairly unchanged all of his life. There may have been a few more buildings added or a new sign, but the changed mood of the night left Greg uninterested in searching for changes in his hometown.

Sitting there, out of control of the bus or the future, Greg decided prayer seemed appropriate and timely. He was never able to reach the prayed ahead status of Chap, but he had gotten pretty good at the in the moment timing.

The bus station in Houston was in a bad part of

downtown. With the news about the assassination surely known, the area could already be a hotbed of tension and perhaps even violence. Greg would take the first local bus out to Melinda's house but call first, just in case.

Ever since the death of Greg's parents, Melinda's mother and even her father had treated him more kindly. Not that they had been unkind before, but sympathy was suddenly mixed into their concern for their daughter and he benefitted from the result.

Greg knew he had things to apologize for doing, but mostly for not doing. Melinda had been great about writing. He had not. He started many letters to her, but the news was either so repetitive that he thought it would be boring or so awful he didn't want to burden her with it. His letters rarely made it to completion, and less often to Melinda herself. He knew he cared about her, even loved her, but how would she know?

In the middle of an operation, for no apparent reason, he would remember some dumb thing he said that made Melinda smile. Then at other times, scary times, he could hardly remember her smile at all. Nights when he couldn't sleep, he tried three things; naming all the John Wayne movies ever made, the starting lineup for the Houston Buffalos 1955-1957, and the times he made Melinda smile.

But would Melinda be smiling when she saw him now? Lots of guys returned home to find everything different. Girlfriends were married. Wives were gone. Lives were gone, neighbors cold, parents hot. Going home was the last thing it should have been after war…untrustworthy.

The air brakes sighed long and then faded as the flat nose of the Greyhound nuzzled the brick wall at the end of the bus's space. Greg grabbed his onboard things and waited outside for the driver to open the luggage area where his large duffel was stored. Things were calmer at the station than Greg had imagined. He slung his large duffle over his right shoulder and as he turned to look for the local bus stop he saw her standing there. Just like the song.

And there was that smile. Greg froze. She was more beautiful than his memories. She stood there in the midst of it all. Humanity of every kind swirled around her but all but he saw was Melinda, dark shiny hair, amazing green eyes, and a short velvet dress.

Her image flashed like the photographer's strobe light on prom night. It flashed like it had in his dreams in Nam. But this time, after the flash, the dream was still alive.

As a quizzical look started to replace her smile, he moved toward her. He wanted to grab her and kiss her like some schmaltzy World War II movie, but awkwardness yelled, *Cut!* in his mind as he reached her.

They stood close and she said, "Welcome home sol-"

Before she could finish, Greg kissed her hard. As hard as Cary Grant or any of those other returning Hollywood soldiers kissed anyone. In mid-kiss Greg thought, *Oh Crap! What if this is the last thing she wanted? Is she kissing me back? How much longer should I-* Then Melinda pulled back, slightly out of breath.

"Hold on there soldier. Give a girl a chance to breathe."

"You shouldn't be here," was the next thing out of his mouth.

"I just couldn't <u>not</u> be here. Besides, Daddy drove me," Melinda said.

Greg instinctively dropped his hold on her.

"He's circling the block," she laughed. "He didn't want to pay to park."

There was that laugh and that great smile. Greg could swim in that smile for days but then he began to notice unfriendly, and some sad and angry faces around them. Greg picked up his duffle and gym bag.

"Is it here?" Melinda gently touched Greg's shoulder.

"'bout there," Greg said.

"Does it hurt?"

"No," Greg lied knowing they needed to start

moving.

"Have you heard about the assassination?" Melinda asked as they walked toward the street to find her father.

"Yes."

"Isn't that just awful? Daddy thinks one of their own might have done it just to keep things stirred up."

He would, Greg thought as he guided her with his hand on her soft back in the velvet dress. Looking down at the gym bag he thought, *I'm dead.*

"There he is. Daddy!" Melinda waved as the two-toned Buick Sport Wagon pulled up 14 inches from the curb to not damage the thin whitewalls. Melinda's father rolled down the passenger side window.

"Mel, you get in here, and I'll pop open the back for your things." Melinda's father instructed Greg. He kept his gym bag with him as he climbed into the back seat moments before Melinda's father pulled away from the curb.

"Terrible part of town. Especially at this time of night."

"Thanks for picking me up," Greg said.

"Well, I sure wasn't going to let my daughter come down here by herself. Have you heard about all the problems going on?"

"Yes sir," Greg said militarily.

"Greg just got back from Vietnam, Daddy. I think he has had plenty of problems of his own for now."

"Of course. I'm sorry Greg. Welcome home. Are we dropping you at your aunt's house?"

"Daddy, you know Mom has a home cooked meal for Greg to welcome him home," Melinda reminded her father.

Melinda's mother's cooking, oh boy, the sarcasm mocked within.

"I knew that, but I thought since it's getting late Greg had probably eaten on the way in. I hear some of those bus stop diners have the best food in the country."

"I don't want to be a bother," Greg said insincerely.

"Nonsense," Melinda said, "Mother would be crushed."

Melinda's father reached for the radio knob in the center of the dashboard, "Just gonna check on the Astros." There was nothing on any station except news reports on the assassination of Dr. Martin Luther King, Jr.

On the way to Melinda's house, Melinda's

father passed by the exit to Tommy's house.

At the same time Greg enlisted or be drafted, Tommy decided he was going into Military Intelligence. He too, went to the same post office where Greg was sworn in and followed suit. But then before he shipped out, in an odd event that could only happen to Tommy, he wrecked his knee in a freak accident crossing busy Houston Avenue on his way to his father's shutter shop to say good-bye.

As things often happened only to Tommy, he was going to be discharged from the service before he even left for Boot Camp.

Greg heard he was going to take his disability money and move to Las Vegas to become a Black Jack dealer at the Stardust. He never heard directly from Tommy again.

Melinda's father snapped off the radio. "You know they are going to blame poor George Wallace for this. And his wife is so sick with cancer. You watch, those... people will be out for his blood for sure."

Greg slid his right foot under Melinda's side. He lifted her seat cushion with his dress shoe enough to let her know he was still back there. Greg looked into the rearview mirror for a reaction but all he saw was her father's unamused puss staring back.

As Melinda's father pulled the Sport Wagon into the drive of their Middle American home, Greg could see Melinda's mother at the window. She stepped out on the small front porch where Greg had kissed

Melinda good night for the first time a lifetime ago. Melinda's mother waved like Ellie Mae on the *Beverly Hillbillies*. Melinda's father popped the rear gate and Greg grabbed his duffel.

"Hi there, Soldier Boy," Melinda's mother shouted from the porch. "We prayed for you every night," she added.

"Thank you. Melinda told me." Greg said.

"I've got dinner ready for you," Melinda's mother said as the three approached the front porch.

"About time, I'm starving," Melinda's father answered walking ahead of Greg and on into the house. *You can have mine*, Greg thought.

Over his shoulder Melinda's father asked, "You heard the Astros' score? Only thing on the radio was trash about that trouble maker," as he entered the front door ahead of Greg."

"Doesn't Greg look great Mother?" Melinda asked as they reached her.

"He sure does. A regular Robert Redford in uniform. How's the-" Melinda's mother hadn't changed. She couldn't ask directly about Greg's wound.

"Fine," Greg soldiered.

"I cannot believe they are going to make you go back. Well, welcome back."

Melinda's mother and Greg awkwardly paused

and tried to figure out their next move. Should Greg put down his olive drab belongings to shake her hand or offer her a hug? Just then she quickly opened the plexiglas outer door for Greg. Melinda followed.

"Just put your camping gear anywhere there in the living room. Just watch if anything has something metal that would scratch. We just had the floors redone," Melinda's mother instructed.

KEN BAILEY

CHAPTER 12

Melinda's House

Greg placed his duffel and small bag on the polished wooden living room floor below the curio cabinet filled with the translucent soft green and blues of her mother's Depression glass collection.

"Melinda Jean, show Greg where he can wash his hands and then come back and help me put things on the table."

"He probably remembers," Melinda smiled at Greg.

"Okay. OH GREG, WOULD YOU USE THE ZEST BAR BESIDE THE SINK? THE LITTLE SOAPS ARE FOR GUESTS," Melinda's mother called out from the kitchen. *Did that mean she thought of him as part of the family or just wasn't special enough for the guest soap?*

When Greg returned from the guest bath, Melinda's Dad and a young man were sitting at the table. The young man got up and with a big smile said, "Welcome home hero!" The young man held out his hand and Greg took it to shake.

Melinda doesn't have a brother or sister so who is this? Greg thought. *Kind of late for a neighbor to drop by and why is he sitting at the table with Melinda's father?*

"Oh good," Melinda's mother said entering with the salad. "You've met – oh the Jell-o, fiddlesticks! – sorry Joshua."

The young man, apparently Joshua, smiled and said, "Think nothing of it Betsy."

Betsy. Maybe it is a cousin on <u>*Betsy's*</u> *side come to visit,* Greg Joe Fridayed. *But why would she be apologizing to a young cousin?*

Melinda followed with a pitcher of iced tea and began filling glasses as her mother entered with a large plate of jiggling lime Jell-O with something suspended inside.

"Wonderful!" Betsy exclaimed. "Greg, you sit here at our seat of honor at the head of the table. I'll sit here." Melinda's mother sat on Greg's right leaving the only open chair between Joshua and her father.

Wait a minute, Greg thought as he smiled and mounted the seat of honor farthest away from Melinda.

"Josh, would you say Grace for us?" Melinda's father asked.

"It would be an honor. Let's hold hands," Joshy the intruder said. Melinda reached out her left hand to her father and her right to Joshua. Melinda shot an uncomfortable glance toward Greg but he was too busy dealing with Josh's outstretched right hand to notice.

Greg thought about giving "Joshy's" hand a

manly squeeze but a prayer was not the right time and Greg's left shoulder from the wound, even with the rehab, did not give his left hand its former strength. Greg uncomfortably reached out his strong, now sweaty right hand, to Melinda's mother. He was just not ready to think of her as Betsy.

"Isn't this nice?" Betsy said and then bowed her head.

"Almighty God. We come together hand in hand, thanking you for this wonderful home and this wonderful smelling meal cooked with loving hands," Josh had only begun.

Aww c'mon, Greg thought as one of those loving hands gently squeezed Greg's with delight.

"And thank you for the return of Greggy here. Wounded, but healed by you, to return to us to accomplish whatever assignment you have for him to do. And thank you for Gerald's faithfulness and-"

GERALD! Greg thought loudly as he tuned out the next, what seemed like thirty-five minutes, of Joshy prayer until-

"and thank you for Melynd and her heart for our children. "

OUR CHILDREN! WHAT THE FUGAZZI? Greg was now completely out of fellowship and ready to punch prayer boy. He was also not that crazy about MELYND at that point either.

"And All God's Children said,"

"Amen!" all chimed in varying degrees of energy and holiness.

"Did they tell you Josh is the Youth Pastor at Mountainview?" Melinda asked honor-seated Greg. Melinda could tell Greg was not home-coming-thrilled with the strange situation.

"Hmm," was all Greg could muster.

"Josh did you catch the final score of the Astros?" Melinda's father asked while putting two pork chops on his plate.

"5 to 4 Astros. The Pirates knocked Dierker around some but he got the win. That crazy Rusty Staub got two hits." Josh said.

"How did you get all that? I couldn't get anything but news about that Rebel Rouser," Gerald complained.

"Now Gerald, we've talked about that," Josh schooled.

"Yes Daddy, it's <u>rabble</u> rouser."

"No, Melynd," then he looked over at Gerald. "I called a friend from Baylor who works on the Sports Desk at the Post. I knew you would want to know."

Baylor, Mountainview Baptists, correcting 'Gerald' - it was all becoming more clear to Greg.

Melinda was right, he should <u>not</u> have dropped Old Testament and should have stayed at Baylor.

"So Greggy," Josh, the evening's de facto Master of Ceremony started.

"I prefer Greg," Greg proffered.

"Oh sorry, Greg of course. How long you back for?"

"Not really sure. It's medical leave. They tell me after some more tests," Greg said.

"Did you see a lot of action over there besides your... accident?" Josh attempted to keep the conversational ball in the air.

"Oh it was no accident Reverend. The little rabble rouser aimed right at me."

Sensing Greg's attitude, Joshua changed his.

"I'll make you a deal. You don't call me Reverend and I won't call you Greggy."

Melinda's mother sensing it was time for a break in the action announced, "Melinda, pass the Jell-o mold around." Melinda picked up the platter of wiggling transparency and offered it to Josh.

"This looks delicious, Betsy. Are those apple pieces in there?"

"Zucchini," Betsy answered proudly. "It seemed healthier and I wanted something healthy for Greg's first night back."

"Oh, thank you, B-" Greg said, completely void of thanksgiving and simply unable to call Melinda's mother Betsy. To increase the discomfort "Betsy" did not insist he call her by the Joshy name either.

As Greg forked the mélange of mystery meat and vegetables Melinda said, "Dad gave Mother a crock pot for Christmas and she has become the Queen of Crockpottery. Would you like to see it, Greg?" Melinda asked.

Taking any chance available to escape the new rice paddy of Melinda's dining room, Greg jumped up.

"Melinda, Greg hasn't even finished. Let the boy eat," her mother said.

"Sit down, Greg, and tell us about it," Gerald said.

Greg wasn't completely sure what _it_ was. He was not going to tell this batch of Baptists how he had committed to publish a book that would crush them. He was not going to tell them about his second black friend who died in his arms, or about trying to sew up young men destroyed by politicians driven by interest beyond his own. So, he told them the self-effacing story of losing his pants to a cactus in New Mexico. Everyone laughed, especially Joshy.

Then Joshua tried to top Greg with a story about his first pastorate in a small Texas town near Waco while he was still in seminary. But the butt of the story was an old black man and the hero of the story was surprisingly, Joshy.

Greg pretty much hated Joshy from that moment on.

The phone rang and Betsy got up to answer it. Josh stood and Greg followed. Melinda's father looked at the two young studs like they were crazy. When they sat back down, Melinda sprung up to get coffee from the kitchen and to see if she could make them stand again. They did. Any young woman would enjoy this kind of attention and she did.

"Josh, did I tell you I was in the National Guard?" Melinda's father volunteered as Greg and Josh returned to their seats.

"Really, Gerald? No, you never told me that." Josh said.

You never told me your name was Gerald, Greg thought.

"Yeah, I was one of the lucky ones. I was assigned to the 144th Army Infantry Regiment. It was called 'Fourth Texas' from its beginnings, even before the Mexican War," Josh's friend Gerald revealed.

"But we're talking WWII, right General?" Josh kissed upward.

General Gerald laughed, "I was no General."

Melinda re-entered the dining room with the coffee pot and motioned for the boys to stay seated.

"Josh?" Melinda asked as she poured for Josh and her Dad. Melinda's mother entered at the same time from the hallway. Melinda's mother held out her cup. Greg then surprised Melinda by holding out the last empty cup on the table. Neither of them drank coffee before Greg went away. Greg still was not big on it, but now was not the time to not participate.

"Did we miss anything?" Melinda's mother asked.

"Just sharing war stories," the M.C. said.

"Oh, did you tell them about guarding Pensacola Beach?" Betsy asked Gerald.

"What?" Josh said.

"Mom," Melinda defended.

"He got real sunburned. And with his completion, I still worry about skin cancer."

"I <u>said</u> I was one of the lucky ones. Many of the soldiers from the 144st served valiantly in both theaters. But I was just not one of them. After VJ day they inactivated the regiment and we simply went home."

"You were truly blessed by God, Brother Gerald," Josh holied up.

"What about you Greg? Besides your wound, you must have seen a lot of atrocities, being a medic."

Josh moved Brother Gerald down the imaginary Carson couch to interview his next guest.

"I have seen atrocities over there and back here." Greg was not a good guest for this audience.

After a moment Melinda's father asked, "So Joshua, speaking of battles do you think this Martin Luther thing is going to disrupt the Convention?"

"We simply can't let it. Especially since it's here."

"Yeah, of all the years to finally be in Houston," Melinda's father added.

"It is going to be a true blessing," Josh continued.

"Do you think the good doctor is really going to be elected President?" Gerald asked.

"I think he has a really good shot. We've all made a lot of phone calls to our friends and-"

Melinda explained, "They are talking about Dr. Criswell from First Baptist Dallas. He is running for President of the Southern Baptist Convention in two months and it's being held here in Houston for the first time in ten years. Everyone at HBU is very excited. I have been assigned two committees and I'm getting credit for one of them."

"Oh Greg, that was Breeze on the phone," Melinda's mother said.

Greg looked confused and Melinda's mother smiled. "I mean your Aunt Brenda."

"That kook, she calls herself Breeze now. Some kind of hippie-baloney."

"Daddy!" Melinda said, "She is not a kook. She had a genuine epiphany when that dog got hit by that Thunderbird."

"Rusty?" Greg asked, "Rusty's dead?"

"No, he's okay. That's the miracle." Melinda said.

"Well, hardly a miracle Melynd," Joshua corrected.

Shut your prayer-hole, jerk, Greg thought.

"Well anyway, Brenda has wanted to be called Breeze since then. She asked if you could stay here tonight and she will pick you up in the morning."

"Is she okay?" Greg asked.

"I'm sure she's fine," Melinda's mother assured him.

"Probably fertilizing her basement pot farm tonight. Fifty-year-old Hippie. Absolutely Ridiculous!" Gerald grunted. Greg did not want to stay there but sleeping in a room near Melinda made the choice easier.

Josh stood to leave. He shook Gerald's hand, "Brother Gerald," and then Greg's, "Welcome home again. We are very proud of you."

"Well, it's certainly been another wonderful evening with you good people." Josh said as he kissed Betsy on the cheek. "Thanks for another great meal. Zucchini in Jell-O. Only you would have thought of that."

"Melinda, walk Joshua out and then meet me upstairs to put fresh sheets on the guest room bed for Greg," Betsy sweetly ordered.

Greg had not been invited upstairs at Melinda's house, ever.

"Here you go," Betsy tour-guided. "It's only got a little half-bath, so to shower you'll have to coordinate with Melinda."

Greg looked at Melinda, who was staring at the oak floor that she had walked on since she was a toddler.

"Melinda, say goodnight and let Greg get ready for bed?"

"In just a minute, Mama."

"Don't dawdle, school night."

Greg stared at Melinda until Betsy reached the bottom step.

Greg ventriloquized through a clinched teeth smile, "Looks like we're neighbors. Know what the Bible says about neighbors?"

"What?" Melinda played dumb.

"So are you and Joshy…?" Greg teased with his heart in his throat.

"It's Reverend Joshy to you, soldier boy," Melinda continued the kidding.

"Which one is your room again?"

"You know where my room is. You tried to get in there plenty of times."

From downstairs Betsy called, "Melinda Jean, say goodnight."

Greg was briefly reassured by a genuine goodnight kiss.

The hot shower felt great on Greg's bus-ridden, Jello-O consumed body. He cupped his hands and stayed "underwater" for what seemed like a collegian record. When he came up for air he remembered his vision of how his homecoming with Melinda would be. He had the time to create many scenarios, both good and bad. This was not one of them.

But the reality was he had no idea of what was next. It sounded like his sweet double-fudge-brownie-baking aunt was now his Hippie brownie-baking aunt. He had no idea how he was going to get Chap's book published and if anyone, including Melinda, would ever talk to him if he did.

But standing there in the warm water he began to think.

"Don't use up all the hot water," Brother Gerald banged on the door.

Shut Up! Rebel Rouser! he thought. But what Greg did was turn off the water and sit down in the couple of inches of warm water that was slowly draining out of the tub and prayed his kind of way.

After he and God had a brief discussion with Greg doing all the talking, he dried off with a non-guest towel. Somewhere around his right anterior fourth rib Greg thought, *it could be worse after all, Melinda was...just down the hall.*

As Greg lay there in someone else's bed, his mind raced all around the room. Questions jumped off walls, out of closets, from the Jesus picture over the clock, and from under the bed.

Questions like, *Has Melinda changed? Have I changed? Why is Jesus staring at me? Why do I suddenly not like the Astros? Is the Southern Baptist Convention really going to elect that guy in Chap's book? No one would serve leftover Zucchini Jell-O for breakfast, would they?*

There was a gentle knock on the door. Greg didn't know if he should put on his robe or not. Then he realized he didn't have a robe. He quietly got out of bed and cracked the door to be greeted by Melinda's smile. She was wearing a blue robe.

Melinda whispered, "Just wanted to say goodnight, again." Melinda hadn't seen the grown up Greg without his shirt and with the scar. His chest and abs looked nothing like the boy she swam with at Linder Lake.

"Glad you did," Greg's chest said.

"Need anything?" Melinda asked.

Greg paused.

"Very funny," Melinda said knowing the answer.

"I'm okay. There is one thing I need to tell you," Greg whispered as he pulled her into the room.

"Greg, not a good idea," Melinda said holding on the door's edge. But then she saw Greg's face lose the playful expression and get serious. "What is it?" Melinda asked seriously.

Greg told her as briefly as he could, leaving out the blood and gore, about Chap, and that he had written a book. He told her about his promise to Chap. He did not tell her the subject or how it might impact Baptists everywhere.

Melinda heard a noise and cracked Greg's door enough to see a clear coast. She told Greg they would talk more but she had to get back to her room.

Once Melinda was back on the hallway side of the door, she leaned in and Greg opened the door back wider. They kissed a long, deep, warm goodnight. And the best news, no porch light. Greg had finally made it onto her father's side of the door. Melinda started to leave and Greg started to close the door but then hoarsely whispered, "Melinda?"

She stepped back to the cracked doorway. "Yes?"

"I found your Dad's magazine stash of naked Methodists under the mattress." And then there it was. Melinda's special big smile escaped before her hand could keep it prisoner. Now he could sleep.

KEN BAILEY

CHAPTER 13

Next morning

Greg was never so glad to see toaster strudel in his life. Melinda's father rolled the small portable television into the doorway so he could watch it from the dining room. Melinda walked in, dressed in her summer church volunteer walking shorts and pink top. "No classes today?" Greg asked.

"No Friday classes this semester," Melinda answered.

"Shh," her father noised.

The television picture was warming up, but the sound was already clear. "Good morning, I am Hugh Downs and today is Friday April 5th. Dr. Martin Luther King, Civil Rights Leader, Nobel Prize Winner, and apostle of non-violence died violently last night in Memphis, Tennessee."

Betsy tipped-toe in with the unfinished platter of Jello-O but miraculously and thankfully it jiggled off the plate and on to the freshly stained hardwood.

"Oh, no!" Melinda's mother exclaimed.

"SSSHHHH!" Brother Gerald exclaimed back.

"The impact of his murder upon America and upon the world is of such proportion that we are devoting our entire program to an examination of his life, his death, and the effect his passing-"

Betsy pushed hard on the swinging kitchen door to get a cloth to clean up her mess.

Gerald unhappily shot out, "Great. Our whole lives have to be put on hold because a Negra gets shot."

"SSHHHH!" Betsy scolded returning with a roll of paper towels. Gerald did not appreciate her return volley.

Hugh Downs continued, "We'll start with the news and here is Frank Blair –"

"I like Frank Blair. I bet he's Baptist," Melinda's mother said from the floor.

Frank Blair reported, "There is shock, anger and humiliation in America this morning, because of the assassination of Dr. Martin Luther King. In some Negro ghettos there was looting."

"Any excuse to grab a TV. Look at that," Gerald lowered the boom with his blood pressure rising.

"-But most Americans, Black and White, were left in a mood of quiet indignation. At this hour the police and the FBI still have been unable to find the man believed to be white-"

"Of course, you tell'm, Commie journalist. Had to be a white guy. Next they'll be showing pictures of George Wallace."

"-Dr. King while he stood on a hotel balcony last evening. President Johnson and Vice President Humphrey,"

"Great now those two monkeys are in the act."

"Gerald, please. Show some respect," Betsy insisted.

"-Expressed the nation's sense of horror and pleaded for an end to bigotry."

Melinda's father got up, walked over and started to hit the off button hard.

"Look," Melinda said, "It's Pastor Dothan."

"They must have brought him into the studio here," Gerald said. "Now we'll get the straight truth."

The camera went to a local anchor who introduced Dr. Dothan from Mountainview Baptist Church in Houston. Before the interview started, Greg heard a horn. With Melinda and her family glued to the portable set, Greg went to the window and saw his Aunt Brenda in a 1959 red and white Volkswagen bus with the tailpipe tied to the back bumper with an extension cord.

Greg had brought his duffle down earlier. He picked it up just as she honked again. He stepped to the dining room doorway, but when he saw Dothan was still being interviewed he slipped out. He would come back and thank them and say his goodbyes after he threw his stuff in the van.

Before he got halfway back up the front walk, Melinda and her mother were on the front porch. They each waved at Brenda, Greg said his goodbyes and asked them to pass along his thanks to Melinda's father.

When Greg got into the passenger seat he could see just how much his Aunt Brenda had changed in two years. The cropped, weekly hairdo was now long, flowing and naturally gray. She did not have a flower in it but she could have. Her dress was long, simple and cotton.

She was genuinely glad to see "Greggy," but like everyone but Joshua, she could tell he was not "Greggy" any longer. She apologized for not picking him up and for not being home when he called.

He told her he enjoyed staying over and getting to see Melinda.

"Did Betsy cook?" she asked.

Greg nodded and they both smiled. Gone was the sorrow and aloneness he saw in her eyes when he left. He wasn't sure if she was happy or stoned or both.

She wasn't stoned. Not because she wouldn't like to have been, but because she discovered she was allergic. "Ain't that a kick in the teeth?" she said in a very un-Aunt Brenda sort of way. Then she laughed. A big, hearty, don't-give-a-damn laugh and then got suddenly sullen.

"You heard about Martin, right?"

Greg thought she was talking about the assassination but she used to date a guy years ago and his name could have been Martin. Greg nodded silently. He figured if she was talking about Dr. King they were in sync, but if she was talking about Martin the plumber the nod would spare him the details.

"I heard Rusty got hit," Greg said.

"He did, Greggy." They were both younger again. "It was weird. Straight out of The Twilight Zone. He's like lying there. I see his spirit rise out of him about....oh, almost eight feet. I start to bawl and then swoosh! It zooms right back into him. He jumps up, pees on Mr. Leonard's lawn elf and runs back to the house. Weird. Am I right?"

Like... swoosh... am I right? Greg thought maybe Rusty's spirit zoomed back into her.

"Want Jack in the Box?" she asked.

"Sure," he said. It was awfully early for a cheeseburger but Jack in the Box had not been opened long in Houston when he left and the toaster strudel was wearing off. The old VW bus wheeled up to the talking clown head.

"Wel-cam- t- ack Box."

"Sputs, is that you?"

"Breeze? What's shakin' bacon?"

"You still trying to make people think your microphone don't work?"

"Gotta do my thang, baby. It's boring as all get out otherwise. What can I do you for?"

"Gimme the usual times two."

"You prego or got company?"

"Company. Say hi to my nephew Greg."

"What's up Greg?"

"Hey there," Greg returned the amicable greeting as an impatient driver behind them laid on the horn.

"Hold your horses, Corvair, or I'll Ralph Nader your butt, just to see the show!"

This has got to be Breeze talking. What have you done with my sweet Aunt? Greg thought.

When they pulled up to his Aunt Brenda's or Breeze's house, he couldn't believe it. The once pristine flowerbeds that often sported the "Yard of the Month" sign were now overgrown and thirsty. The trim on the house needed painting. Greg would like to do that for her while he was home if his shoulder could handle it.

Greg carried the hamburger bag and drinks up the walk. The front door was unlocked. Breeze leaned into it to open. The Texas ground had settled and the door drug on the entry tile. There was a fan-shaped design from repeated openings and closings.

"A Whiter Shade of Pale" played on a really good stereo somewhere.

"Anybody home?" Breeze shouted.

He wasn't sure if she was kidding or not.

"Down here," someone responded.

Down here. There is no down here in a Houston house, Greg thought.

At less than 50 feet above sea level on a good day, basements in Houston homes were as rare as Dallas Cowboy banners.

Aunt Brenda could see Greg's confusion but chose not to attempt an explanation. Instead she took the fast food from him and told Greg to put his things in his old room.

The hallway light was out. He felt along the wall until he came to hanging beads where the door for his room used to be. Beyond the beads the windows must have been covered or painted black for it to be as dark as it was on a bright Houston morning. He dropped his duffel and a small lamp flicked on. A young woman in a Steppenwolf t-shirt unwound off Greg's old twin bed.

"Who are you, man?" she asked.

Before he could answer, Aunt Brenda walked in with a flashlight.

"What are you doing in here?" Aunt Brenda/Breeze asked the girl.

"Tumbo said I could crash here. I worked last night and my old man forgot to pick me up."

"Well, you can't stay in here. This is Greg's room."

"Okay, okay. Don't have a conniption. I'm going." She yanked on her pants that were laying on the floor where she had stepped out of them, and she was out the door within seconds.

"I've asked Tumbo twenty times to replace that hall light. Here take this." Aunt Brenda handed him the flashlight. "Food's in the kitchen. Wash up and we'll eat."

Greg worked his way down the flashlight lit hallway to the bathroom. He knocked on the door and opened it when no one answered.

The bathroom, unlike the rest of the house, was exactly like it was when he left. The light switch worked and the sink had hot and cold water. A clean hand towel was hung neatly over the long bar between the sink and the shower and he could use any soap he wanted. He was home, sort of.

Greg joined his aunt at the table in the kitchen. She had put paper towels down and had opened the cheeseburgers and packets of secret sauce and dumped the fries' next to the sandwich. A large bottle of Hunt's Ketchup was in the middle of the table. Just as Greg sat, a large shadow covered the entire tabletop. Without looking behind he knew that had to be Tumbo.

"Greg, this is Tumbo."

He turned to shake Tumbo's hand but the huge Wolfman Jack looking creature drew back. He had black paint or something like plaster beyond his wrists and spackled up both forearms enough to make shaking hands messy.

"Wash up," Aunt Brenda ordered.

Greg realized the other cheeseburger and fries were Tumbo's.

"He helps me out here," she explained.

Tumbo walked out back and did not use the clean bathroom.

After the burgers, fries, and Tumbo were gone, Aunt Breeze, as Greg had decided to think of her, sat down.

"How are you really, Greggy?" she asked.

Greg told her the truth about Vietnam, Chap, and his injury. But not about the book. Aunt Breeze gave him a great homecoming gift. She just listened.

Now it was Greg's turn. He wanted to know how a sweet, quiet Aunt Brenda became Breeze, a Tumbo-employing, Steppenwolf t-shirted Goldilocks boarding, blacked out windowed, non-dope-smoking hippie. So he asked, "What's new with you?"

Before she could answer there was a knock at the door.

"Get down!" Aunt Breeze said fearfully.

Greg, with too much My Tho River still in his blood, dove immediately under the table.

"Shh," Aunt Breeze whispered as she eased up and headed for the door.

Greg saw her grab something off a shelf when she walked by it. Was it a gun? Or drugs? Was Aunt Breeze a dope dealer?

"Oh, hi!" Greg heard her say at the door. "C'mon in."

He heard Melinda's voice and banged his head on the table bottom as he jumped to his feet. Melinda entered holding Greg's gym bag.

"Hi," Melinda said to Greg.

She looked as great in the daylight as she did at the bus station.

"I thought you might need this," Melinda said holding out the gym bag. Greg remembered he had left it in their shared bathroom and that he had not returned his shaving supplies to it.

"Thanks, I do." Greg said.

"Wanna go for a ride?" Melinda asked coyly.

"Sure." A day with Melinda would be amazing. He knew that within minutes he would actually know where he stood with her. How much of a threat Josh was. And with a little luck they could find a place to make-out and she would want to as much as he did.

Greg got into the passenger side of her high-school graduation gift. Melinda walked around to the driver's side and waved to Aunt Breeze at her door.

"Bye," Melinda said as she entered behind the wheel. Aunt Breeze closed her door and Melinda boomed, "ARE YOU CRAZY?"

"What?" he shocked back.

"WHAT ARE YOU DOING WITH THAT BOOK IN YOUR BAG?"

Images of a pleasant coffee house conversation and a nooner make-out session disappeared instantly.

"Could we just go somewhere and talk? I'll explain everything," he answered.

Melinda silently drove the nine blocks to the Pig Stand. There were only three cars there when they arrived. She ordered a Coke, no pineapple, and Greg just wanted water. His mouth was suddenly very dry.

He did not want to lead with, "You shouldn't have gone into my bag without my permission." That would not set the constructive tone he was going for and besides he had left it in her bathroom unzipped and sticking out like a flag on a rural mail box.

Her body language and lack of talk told him if he started from the beginning, her frozen mood would not be thawed in time for the explaining part. Leading with a joke was out of the question. So, he started by slowly rotating his wounded shoulder and wincing slightly hoping for a little sympathy, which did not happen.

"You remember the last time we were here?" he said to no response.

The nostalgia card trumped nothing.

"Okay, here's the deal. I promised a guy I would try and get that book published."

"That book?"

"Yes."

"Published?"

"Yes."

"What do you know about publishing a book?"

"Nothing. So I figured there is no way-"

"Who's this guy? And why would you promise to publish such a book of lies?"

"It's not lies."

"Really?"

"Yes."

"Get out of my car."

"What?"

"You heard me. Get out of my car."

Melinda laid rubber squealing out of the Pig Stand parking lot.

"Hey, she's got my Coke glass. I have to pay for that," the carhop complained to Greg as he watched the yellow Camaro race away. He was at once impressed by her driving and crestfallen to see her go.

Greg took almost an hour to walk back to Aunt Breeze's. Along the way he decided to forget about the book. Melinda was right. He didn't know the first thing about how to get a book published. It would be ridiculous to even try. Chap would understand.

When he got home he saw a police car outside. He expected to see his Aunt being brought out in handcuffs but by the time he made it to the front door he had seen nothing. He opened the door cautiously and heard Aunt Breeze laughing.

He entered the kitchen and saw Aunt Breeze drinking iced tea with a cop sitting facing her.

"Hi, Greg. Look who dropped by," Aunt Breeze said.

When the officer turned, Greg was shocked to see it was Tommy.

"Hey, Numb Nuts." Tommy said.

Tommy's move to Vegas never happened. He had to go in for another physical and the Army found his knee would be okay for service in less than six months. During that time Tommy made a deal with them that if he completed the Police Academy they would let his discharge go through. He had been on the Houston Police force for over a year.

"You remember," he said, "At Reagan you either become the bad guys or lock 'em up. Hell, half the force are old Bulldogs."

Greg and Tommy visited long enough for him to get a robbery-in-progress call.

"Gotta' jet," he said and was off like the Lone Ranger. Greg was amazed. He had always pictured Tommy as Tonto.

Even with the joy of Tommy's surprise visit, Aunt Breeze could tell Greg was unhappy. When she asked him what was wrong he told her about Melinda, the book and his decision to give up on his promise.

"What's in this book?" she asked.

Greg told her. Then she told him a story.

It seems after Rusty became her miracle pup, she adopted a stray cat. The cat was therapy for Rusty and the two got along surprisingly well. One day the cat went missing. Aunt Breeze was afraid natural instincts had kicked in and Rusty harmed his little friend. But

Rusty was sad. Breeze could tell he missed his friend. One day she came home and Rusty was scratching at the baseboard of the cedar-lined closet in the back hallway. At first Breeze thought maybe he had cornered a mouse but there was no mouse there. She got down on her hands and knees and realized there was a small break in the floorboard that outlined what could have been a three-foot square trapdoor. She got to her feet and wedged the bend of an empty coat hanger in the space and leveraged it up enough to get slide in two fingers and then her hand. Pulling upward it hinged open easily and Rusty's feline friend ran out. Rusty was delighted.

Breeze shined a flashlight into the opening and found it was a bomb shelter built by the old man who had owned the house before her. Once down the ladder she found old wooden crates of canned goods, a gas mask, and a few risqué postcards from World War I.

"Would you like to see it?" Aunt Breeze asked.

On their way to the cedar closet Greg asked, "How did the cat get in there?"

"There was an airshaft that was somehow stuck open and the cat must have fallen in it," she said.

When Aunt Breeze reached up and pulled a string attached to the base of a naked bulb in the closet ceiling, a light in the shelter lit at the same time. A lumber jack's axe was driven into the cedar wall and holding the trapdoor open. *That had to be Tumbo's work,* he thought. He and his aunt climbed down a narrow, sturdy Tumbo-built stairway. Everything in the shelter from the old man was gone. It had been replaced by an A. B. Dick 360 offset printing press. Strewn around and on shelves were copies of something called, *The Cosmic Catacombs*.

"Have you heard of the C.C.?" Aunt Breeze asked.

He shook his head "no" as he picked up a copy dated March 23, 1968 with a headline, *Down with Dowling*. The article encouraged concerned lovers of justice and peace to picket the statue of the Confederate local white hero, Dick Dowling, in Emancipation Park.

"Have you heard of The Rag?" Aunt Breeze asked.

Greg had not. She explained The Rag was an underground free press newspaper in Austin and that it had gained some national notoriety for some of its establishment subversive content. She told him the Cosmic Catacombs was like that only published here in her bomb shelter. She said the FBI and other authorities have been looking everywhere to find out where it is printed.

Once again Greg envisioned his aunt being carted off in handcuffs.

"But Greggy, don't you get it? We can print your book!"

Oh crap! Now I have no excuse for Melinda, Greg thought.

Greg was sure this was an answer to one of Chap's prayed ahead prayers. He was also sure he no longer had a prayer with Melinda. He figured somewhere Joshy is being thankful for a gift he did not even know he was given.

There was no turning back now. Greg would get Chap's manuscript into Tumbo's inky hands and this chapter in his life would be closed. He would move on to get a medical release and return to active duty before the Southern Baptist Convention convened.

KEN BAILEY

CHAPTER 14

Texas Medical Center

Greg drove his aunt's VW van up to the glaring stare of the security guard in the Medical Center parking lot.

Once he parked and found his way into the medical building, Greg pulled a note from his pocket and took an elevator to the fourth floor.

"Greg Henderson to see Dr. Big... I mean Dr. Bigalow."

"Would you sign here, please, and take a seat over there?" the attractive Black woman in civilian clothes said.

Greg started to do as she asked and then felt the need to explain, "I'm sorry, Dr. Big was what we called him in-"

Greg could see she was unimpressed and too business-like to care about war buddies and war stories even if she knew Bigs was in Vietnam during some rough days and nights.

But then he realized her business-like demeanor was actually covering up tears. Greg spotted the Houston Chronicle under her appointment book. She had been reading about the assassination of someone that was undoubtedly very important to her. Greg wanted to reach out and console her. He wanted to say,

"My best friend in 'Nam was Black." But that sounded wrong even in his thoughts. He wanted to tell her that he had been entrusted with an important manuscript by a man who had given his life for her but that would sound more like Jesus than Chap.

He wanted to tell her his best friend Chap, who was just about the same color as her wet cheek, was greatly inspired in his personal ministry and military life by Dr. King. But Chap and Greg had never discussed Martin Luther King and Greg had no idea how Chap actually felt about the martyred Civil Rights leader.

He wanted to tell her what Chap would be doing about all this if he were alive. But then Greg thought, *How do I know what Chap would be doing if he were still alive?* Greg suddenly realized how little he really knew about his friend when the receptionist asked, "Was there something else you needed?" Greg shook his head *no* and gave her his best empathic look, which in mid-expression Greg knew made him look like he was seeing the wrong kind of doctor.

Instead, Greg crossed to the modern-looking bank of blue chairs mounted alongside others on a chrome crossbeam. He looked over an assortment of well-read magazines on the glass side table and chose a January Time Magazine with a very unflattering drawing of LBJ as Time's Man of the Year on the cover. Inside the four month old publication, several pages had been torn out and someone had drawn a moustache on President Johnson. *Yep, freedom of expression, that's what we were fighting for*, Greg thought.

Greg put down the magazine and waited. Soon the receptionist walked over to him and said, "I'm sorry Dr. Big," she smiled, "has an emergency but said if you do not mind waiting he would love to see you." Returning to her desk she turned back to Greg and whispered loud enough for him to hear ten feet away, "Let's keep the Dr. Big between you and me, okay?" Greg smiled, nodded and then asked, "Did he really say 'love'?"

"Actually I added that," she said. Greg wiped his right hand across his head, "Whew." They both smiled as only professionals can.

Greg spotted a phone on a desk next to a coffee maker.

"Can I make an outside call on that phone?" Greg asked the friendly receptionist.

"Sure. Just punch 9 and then your number."

He got up but before he reached the phone, he heard something he really didn't want to hear.

"Greggy!" the voice from behind him said. Greg turned. It was Reverend Joshua.

"Hey," Greg said. "Small world. What are you doing here?" Greg asked not caring about Josh's answer.

"Oh, I practically live here. We have members here at the Medical Center every day. While my youth are in school I come up here and visit my salary, I mean our senior members." Josh said kiddingly. "Can I buy you a coffee? The clergy get these tokens for free coffee," Josh explained.

"Sure," Greg answered not knowing how long his wait would be.

The two young men walked over to the large coffee machine and Josh dropped in the first token. "It comes out black but you can punch any of the extras over here. I take mine like I like my women, with cream and sugar."

Greg would have preferred punching St. Obnoxious but chose instead to punch cream no sugar.

Then St. O. said, "Hey, I'm sorry about horning in on your homecoming last night."

"That's okay," Greg lied.

"With us hosting the convention here in less than three months and now with the King thing, Dothan has become pretty overwhelmed."

"Really?" Greg asked.

"Yes." Josh motioned for Greg to sit back down on the blue fake-leather chairs. "I wouldn't want this to get around but – The good Doctor is having some… problems and one of the problems is manifesting itself in behaving more... liberal." Greg leaned in even though Josh's intentional stage whispers could be heard in the third floor cafeteria.

"Mountainview, well you know. You used to be a member," Josh said.

"Still am as far as I know," Greg replied.

"No, I've gone through and expunged inactive folks in order to have a more accurate accounting of our voting membership. Well, within this time when our Baptist traditions are being challenged it is important that our leadership reflects and guides the people in making correct choices."

"I see," Greg said.

"During this time when I have felt led to take on more responsibility for Mountainview, Brother Gerald has become a real supporter and with him about to be the new Chairman of the Deacons next Sunday-"

Josh finally said something that surprised Greg followed by a second surprise.

"And then there's Melynd. Betsy and Gerald want me to marry her-"

"Really?"

"Yeah. And I'm thinking seriously about it. There's just a couple of things-"

"Really? Like what?" Greg trapped.

"Oh just things. They wouldn't matter to someone like you but... you know things like- she doesn't play the piano. All I know she can play is the radio. And what she listens to. Like Roy Orbison, I mean, c'mon Roy Orbison?"

"Hard to believe," Greg played along. "What else?"

"Well, I mean she can learn to play the piano or even the organ but - it's that attitude of hers. A preacher's wife, especially a preacher that's going places-"

"Like you?" Greg clarified.

"Exactly. We need our wives to be submissive like the Bible says. And well, Melynd, I mean, have you heard the way she talks to her father some times?"

"Yeah, almost like she has a mind of her own," Greg was starting to really enjoy this.

"But I know for both our good, I can whip her into shape in no time. And speaking of shape, that is not one of her problems, if you know what I mean? But I don't have to tell you. You used to date her in high school, didn't you?"

Greg's enjoyment turned on a dime and then-

"Greg! Good to see you." Dr. Bigalow said as he quickly walked up to Greg and Josh.

Greg and Dr. Big shook hands for a beat longer than usual. "When did you back?" Dr. Bigalow asked.

"Three weeks ago. Just got to Houston yesterday. Oh, this is Reverend Joshua..?"

"Markus," Josh finished. "Pastor Mountainview Baptist Church... Houston."

"I've heard of it," Dr. Bigalow kidded, followed by an uncomfortable moment. "I thought Dr. Dothan was pastor there."

"Yes. He's currently Senior Pastor. Well, like you, I've got sick people to see. Nice meeting you Doc. See ya' Greg," as Josh continued on his way.

"Hmm, seems like a real ass," Dr. Big commented when Josh was out of earshot. "How's the shoulder?" Dr. Bigalow asked.

"It's okay."

"Come on to my office, let's catch up and I'd like to take a look at it."

As they passed by the reception desk Dr. Big asked Greg, "Did you meet Eugenia?" Greg nodded an answer and then smiled at the cute receptionist who seemed in better spirits than when Greg entered an hour or so ago.

"Don't piss off Eugenia or you'll never see a doctor."

Sitting in the chair in front of Dr. Big's desk with the glassy view of the entire Medical Center out the window, Greg was taking it all in when Dr. Big said, "You still thinking about joining our PA program when you get out?"

"Is it up and running yet?" Greg asked.

"Just started our first class of 11 guys a month ago."

Greg rubbed his left shoulder without realizing it.

"Here, come in here." Dr. Big said crossing to a door in his office's side wall. He opened the door into an examining room as Greg followed. "Take off your shirt and let me see it."

Greg complied, and tossed his shirt onto the chair at the foot of the examination table.

"Looks like they did a better job shooting up your shoulder than our boys did fixing it."

"Yeah, you went and left me with the second team," Greg kidded.

"I had to get back here to my practice before they while there was still some of it left. I want to get some pictures of that shoulder, then we will talk some more." Dr. Big opened a far door in his examining room and gave a nurse orders to send Greg to x-ray.

Back from X-ray Greg sat in the waiting room again, but for only a minute this time. Dr. Big walked out and Greg jumped to attention. This action surprised them both. Surgeons and techs in the Air Force rarely practiced any of the officer/enlisted men rituals other military personnel acted out.

"At ease," Dr. Big laughed. "Come on back."

Back in his examining room, Dr. Big and Greg looked at the large backlit x-rays hanging on the wall. "Damn, those guys must have lit up that red nose on their Operation Game twenty times working on you," Dr. Big quipped. "No, actually it's coming along fine. Unfortunately you should be ready to go back over for the rest of your tour when your leave is over."

Greg did not react.

"I'll write a note to the Flight Surgeons over at the VA and get you 30 more days stateside. I'm afraid that's about all I can milk this for."

"Thanks Doc," Greg said. "Great to see you again."

"You too Greg. Let that be the last hole you let them put in you."

The two friends nodded and parted company.

KEN BAILEY

CHAPTER 15

Aunt Breeze's House

It was starting to get dark when he pulled Aunt Breeze's van into her driveway. He grabbed the Church's Chicken box and drink out of the front seat. He pushed on the unlocked door with his good shoulder and went inside.

No aunt, no Tumbo, no Steppenwolf T-shirt, it was just him. Greg had gone from his own room in that house to a barracks with thirty other guys, and now back to an empty room in an empty house.

He could try to call Melinda but she would probably be out with Josh. He could turn on TV and eat his chicken but he wasn't hungry enough yet. He decided to finish Chap's book. After Criswell's sermon, the news of the assassination, and finally reaching Houston, he decided to let it go. Now that it was actually going to get printed, he figured he needed to know all of what everyone would be reading.

He opened the manuscript that had interrupted him and Melinda, took a sip of his Coke, and positioned himself to finish. He picked up where he left off; read a few pages, took a bite out of a drumstick, chomped a couple of fries, and turned to page 114.

Near the middle of 114 the name Houston jumped out. Was it a person or his hometown? It was his Houston in 1955.

A thirteen-year-old
Black boy had been seen
flirting with a white girl. The
girl had come to a brush arbor
service.

Chap explained that a brush arbor service dated back to when slaves on plantations would sneak into the woods or a clearing in the brush to have Bible studies, preaching, and even baptisms. Of course in 1955, no one was hiding from plantation owners. This little group simply did not yet have a church building at the time and it was a beautiful, full-mooned Spring Houston night.

While they were
singing and praising Jesus, the
girl's father burst through the
woods and found his daughter
innocently sharing a Bible and
appearing to be holding hands
with the thirteen-year-old son
of the lay preacher conducting
the service.

Behind the girl's
father was a group of outraged
white men who had been
frantically searching for the
missing girl for over an hour.
Seeing the anger in her
father's eyes and fearing the
worst, she ran off deeper into
the woods. Instead of chasing
his daughter, the father
grabbed the Black child by the
neck and hit him hard. The

*young Black's father rushed to
help his son and someone in
the crowd hit him over the
head with an axe handle.*

*The full moon hid
embarrassed behind nearby
clouds as the out-of-control
mob followed the father as he
punched and drug the boy out
of the woods.*

*A sweaty-from-
looking-everywhere man
rushed to his truck that was
parked in the almost empty
church parking lot. Two Black
women, screaming and crying,
were gathered up by their
waists and held back.*

*The mob moved as one.
No thought was given to
innocence, or justice, or age.
Rage was the only voice heard.
A father's rage against a defiler
of his only daughter, a defiler of
his way of life, a defiler of his
blood heritage. The greasy rope
that had pulled cars and
tractors out of Houston fields
and ditches flew deftly over a
high limb of the old oak near
the church. The helpful rope
had never taken a life, even a
smart-assed, little nigger life.*

*Until that moment. Within that
moment, the mob went silent,
the boy danced under that
Founder's Tree. Someone
finally danced on the grounds of
Mountainview Baptist Church
in Houston, Texas.*

Greg was in shock. Chap knew Greg was from
Houston. Why hadn't he mentioned this? Greg could not
remember discussing Moutainview with Chap, only little
Trinity Street Baptist. But still, did Melinda know this
story? Did her father? Did Dothan? Was this why Melinda
was so upset? For some reason Greg didn't think she read
this far. Was this hurtful enough to not print the book?
Should he just burn it and forget it? And then Greg turned
to page 115. Page 115 had no words, only an
underexposed 5X7 picture of the Founder's Tree and the
young Black boy hanging from it and a brown, 5X7 photo
envelope. Greg opened the envelope. It was the original
Polaroid of the printed image. When Greg looked closely
at the photograph his pupils involuntarily dilated and then
filled instantly with tears. IT WAS EMMETT! Kind,
jack-playing, cowboy-socking, big-smiling, preacher-
listening, Emmett. Greg's first Black friend.

Greg's bad shoulder swung his arm across Aunt
Breeze's kitchen table sending pages everywhere. He got
up and with little Emmett's likeness held tightly he walked
to the cedar closet. Greg's anger pulled Tumbo's axe out
of the cedar wall like Arthur extracting Excalibur from the
stone. The trapdoor slammed shut.

With the Polaroid riding shotgun on the seat beside

him, Greg drove the VW bus to Mountainview. The night was moonless and motionless. He drove the van up to the base of the killing tree. Seething, he got out with the engine running and the headlights focused on the trunk, his shadow struck the tree before the axe. His shoulder was healed… for the moment. The axe blade hit a perfect 45 degree angle into the bark and beyond. Next an upward stroke inversed the angle from the bottom and first blood was drawn. Swing after swing, one from the top, one from the bottom, wedge after splintering wedge hit the dirt around the roots. Pieces of annual rings celebrating picnics, fireworks, new buildings, loan burnings, and a young boy's lynching bit the dust.

But the trunk's diameter was greater than Greg's wounded shoulder. With a huge, probably tree assassinating hunk taken out of it, he got back into the running van. He backed up into the parking space reserved for the Senior Pastor and turned to exit. He then put the hippie van in reverse and backed up to the base of the tree. The flat nose and bumper of the van touched the bark from the uncut side. Putting the VW bus in first gear, he pushed slowly down on the accelerator. Then further and further toward the floorboard his foot pressured. Losing their grip on the parking lot's asphalt, the tires started to spin, squeal and then smoke. Just when it seemed the old tree would win, it started to go. It fell hard and took with it two power lines connected to the church. The broken lines crackled and danced before the first sparks hit the dry tree. The flames could be seen for blocks and blocks within only seconds. Before the killing kindling was halfway consumed, he heard sirens. The first to arrive was a police car. Without realizing it, Greg picked the axe back up.

The cop got out of his car and put his hand on his

holstered gun. Greg tightened his grip on the axe.

"Freeze! What kind of Agent Orange crap is this?" It was Tommy. Greg let the axe fall to the asphalt.

Greg entered the holding cell without incident.

"George Washington, my man," said one of the three Black men already sitting in the cell. Greg did not respond.

The third Black man explained to his two incarcerated brothers, "This is the white boy that cut down that old tree at that big church. What you got against trees, honky?" Greg still did not speak.

"I'm talking to you, sapkilla," the Black man responded in Greg's space. Greg rose, but before either could swing the guard approached.

"Henderson," he said as he put the unlocking key in the plate, "you have a visitor."

"This ain't over Paul Bunyan," the threatening Black man sneered.

Greg walked down the pea green tile hallway. The guard opened the door and Greg scanned the room. Among the families, girlfriends, and lawyers sat Joshua, smiling. Greg started to return to his cellmate fight, but the guard prodded him with a nightstick.

Joshua did not get up when Greg approached. Greg sat. Joshua stared at him for a minute then put the photograph of Emmett on the table.

"I think you left this," he stated. Greg did not respond.

"I convinced Dothan not to press charges." No response.

"When you get out of here you need to head on back. Melynd told me about the book. Just forget the whole thing and the church will not pursue any further action," Joshua said. Greg's pupil's narrowed and Joshua, for the first time, was intimidated by Greg.

"Well, I've got people to see. Just wanted to let you know the good news. Guard you can take him back now."

The guard walked beside Greg and he stood slowly. Joshua made no further eye contact.

Greg walked out of Riesner Street police station into an overcast Houston morning. Breeze's van with Tumbo driving pulled alongside.

"Get in," Breeze said.

Greg sat in the back seat.

"Sorry I wasn't there to get you, Greg, but we had to get the van out of impound."

On the way to her house, Breeze talked about the newspaper article on the events of the past evening. She told Greg that she thought it best if he moved into the YMCA for a few days until things blew over. There was already too much interest in her house and Greg's presence would only make it worse. As they turned her corner she told Greg she had a surprise for him.

When they walked up the front sidewalk, they could see the always unlocked door opened wide. Once inside, Breeze panicked.

"Oh no!" she exclaimed. She ran to the cedar closet.

"OH NO! TUMBO COME HERE."

Greg followed. Everything in the bomb shelter was missing or demolished. The offset printing press was in pieces. Old copies of the *Cosmic Catacombs* were strewn on the floor everywhere.

"It's gone," she told Tumbo and Greg.

"Your book, we finished your book Greggy. It's gone, the plates are gone," Breeze sobbed.

Greg turned and climbed back up the steps.

When he passed through the still wide open front door, he saw Melinda's yellow Camaro pulled up to the curb. He walked directly to it as she got out.

"Give me your keys," Greg ordered quietly. Melinda complied, surprised by Greg's force in demanding. He got behind the wheel as she ran to the passenger side.

"You're not taking my car without me!" she insisted. She opened the passenger door and jumped in as Greg laid rubber peeling away from the curb.

"Don't you want to know why I showed up?"

Greg just drove.

"I was worried about you."

Greg looked over at her for a flash without changing his expression. He arrived at the church within minutes. Greg got out of the car and headed for the door marked, "Church Offices."

"May I help you?" the kind lady behind the chest high counter asked. Greg did not answer but walked down a long hallway. Melinda entered the office.

"Melinda dear. Is everything all right? Should I call-"

"It's okay Martha," Melinda assured as she followed Greg down the hallway.

Greg came to a door with a black nameplate beside it that read, "Reverend Joshua Michaels". Greg opened the door and startled Joshua and Melinda's father in a conference.

"I need to speak with Josh," Greg said quietly to Brother Gerald.

"Daddy," Melinda said just arriving at the doorway.

"You have nothing to say to Joshua-"

"Get out of here now," Greg's sternness cut off and shocked Melinda's father.

"Daddy, let's go."

"I'll be right out here if you need me, Joshua," the elder Gerald mumbled.

Greg closed the door behind them with his left shoe, never taking his eyes off Joshua.

"Where is it?" Greg asked.

"Where's what?"

Greg started to move to Joshua.

"All I have to do is call out and the police will be here and you'll be through. You've already lost Melynd. Your book is history. Do you want to add jail time to your pathetic story?"

"If I'm going to jail it might as well be for beating the crap out of you."

"Wait," the cowardly Joshua said. "If I give you back the book will you promise to wait until the Convention is over before you distribute it?"

"You took his book?" Melinda entered having overheard. Greg backed her out of the room and re-closed the door.

"Give me the book," Greg ordered.

"All right, all right. It's right here." Joshua opened a desk drawer and pulled out a handgun instead of the manuscript.

"You are ruining everything," Joshua said through clenched teeth so as to not be heard outside the door.

"Dothan was starting to turn. He was getting soft on the nigger situation. Our people don't want that. He would be out and I would be in. With Melynd as my future wife, Gerald would be completely on my side. Everything was perfect and it will be again. They saw how you came in here to attack me. A quick self-defense plea and everything is back on track. Say hi to your nigger friends for me."

Greg stepped toward the gun and Joshua blinked. A blink that lasted long enough for Greg to grab the gun and hit Joshua hard enough to send him flying into the Sermon on the Mount diorama on the wall behind him.

The crash caused the door to open again immediately. Greg was holding the gun and Joshua was on the floor. Melinda and her father rushed in with every office worker crowded in the hall behind them. One of the workers screamed when she saw Greg with the gun. Tommy pushed through the crowd and passed Martha who had called him.

"Put the gun down Greg," Tommy said with his own gun drawn.

Greg handed Tommy the gun. Melinda helped

Joshua to his feet.

"Let's go," Tommy ordered Greg.

"Wait," said Melinda's father. "That's not Greg's gun, it's mine. I loaned it to Joshua over a month ago."

"Sorry, I'm going to have to take him in and let a judge sort all this out."

The agitated Black man was not in the holding cell when Greg returned. Two drunks and an Asian guy had better things to do than harass Greg.

The guard returned. "Henderson, you have a visitor."

This time when Greg entered the room of families, girlfriends and lawyers, Joshua was not there. Melinda was not there. Breeze was not there. Greg thought maybe the guard had made a mistake, and then he saw him.

Dr. Dothan was sitting alone at a far table. When he saw Greg, he stood. Greg crossed to him. They sat on opposite sides of the table.

"How are you doing?" Dothan asked. "Not my best question," he continued. "I believe this belongs to you," Dothan said as he extracted a printed copy of Chap's book.

"Where?" Greg asked with his eyes.

"Joshua was kind enough to let me have it," Dothan said with a smile. "It was a parting gift. His parting, not mine. In fact, when you go back in there you may see him."

Sharing a cell with Joshua would be a mixed blessing, Greg thought.

"But you won't be going back in there," Dothan told him. "Greg-" Dothan said. It was surreal to share a table with a man he had only seen thirty feet away behind a giant pulpit who was now calling him by his name. "-I read your friend's book. It wasn't easy. I could argue a few things in there. Did you know I love to argue? Probably a sin but who's counting? Certainly not God at this point. But for the most part, it is sadly true. It's a history many of us know but choose to forget. I like to think we have tried to make up for our wrong thinking by doing the right thing over and over. Like anyone in my position I could list thousands and thousands of acts of love and Christian kindness. But unlike anyone else, I have a strong reason to not see it printed.

"I thought about coming to you and asking you to consider letting me edit it or not publishing it at all. But then I came to this." Dothan turned to page 115. It was hard for Greg to look.

"You see that corner of the church there?" Dothan placed his well-manicured index finger on the picture of Emmett.

Greg stoically stared at Dothan.

"You see that window?" Dothan's eyes began to moisten. "I was standing at that window. Mountainview was the first church that called me to be Senior Pastor. I had only been in Houston three months. I was working late on my sermon. It was ironically the story of Pilate and the trial of Jesus. I heard them at first. Then I saw them. Images of locusts swarming over Egypt went through my recent seminary-educated mind. When I saw the rope thrown over the branch of the Founder's Tree, I yelled but no one heard me through the glass. I ran to the door but when I opened it, it was too late. That young life was gone. The crowd left as quickly as they formed. No one knew I was an eyewitness. I walked out there and stared up at that sweet face contorted by hate. I could not reach high enough to get him down. I thought I would get a ladder and call someone. I walked to the janitor's closet to get a ladder. In the lost and found on a shelf by the ladder was a Polaroid camera. My folks had given me one like it for graduation. It still had film in it. I don't know what possessed me but I took it and the ladder out to the tree. I snapped a picture and pulled the tab. I climbed the ladder and carried him down. There was no blood. Death without blood further skewed reality."

Dothan paused to remember.

"Sometime later before it faded, I showed a cousin the photograph. He asked if he could have it. I knew he wrote for a magazine and I guess I thought an article on the tragedy would be cleansing. I never saw a story and I never asked about it again.

The Founder's Tree became a kind of Calvary to me. Ashamed of my part in not stopping it and a sign of redemption as our unknowing people came to see the tree, not for its pain, but for its promise of steadfastness. Guess once a preacher always a preacher." Dothan smiled.

"Did you know we have a large printing shop at the church?" Dothan changed the tone. "One of the largest in Houston. I would like to print this book and give a copy to everyone coming to the Convention next month. What do you say?"

"I think Chap would like that," Greg said.

"Oh, there's someone outside that would like to see you," Dothan's eyes twinkled.

Greg walked out of Reisner Street police station free for the second time. Melinda's yellow Camaro was at the curb.

She got out of the car and threw Greg the keys. She entered the passenger side and they took off at the posted speed limit.

"I feel like a Pineapple Dr. Pepper," Greg said. Melinda smiled as they headed for the Pig Stand. She leaned her head onto his good right shoulder just as she had when he was leaving for the Air Force. But this time there were no tears.

That Sunday Greg, Melinda, Breeze and Tumbo were at the 11 o'clock Trinity Street Sunday service. But that night Greg reluctantly accepted a personal invitation from Dr. Dothan to attend the Sunday evening service at Mountainview. Going back there, even as a guest of the senior pastor, made Greg wary.

Josh was out on bail. The remains of the Founder's Tree had been chain-sawed and removed. Chap's book was supposedly press-ready. Why did Dothan need Greg back at the church? He was not going to be given the Member of the Year Award.

Greg and Melinda entered from the double doors off the front parking lot. He had no interest in seeing where the Founder's Tree used to be.

Heads turned and voices mumbled as they walked to the second pew from the back. Gerald stood up from his familiar pew near the front and motioned for Greg and his daughter to join him. This would mean Greg was trapped. Melinda looked at him for direction. Greg rose and walked down to Brother Gerald. Betsy scooted over to make room for her daughter and Greg. He waited for Gerald to sit but he whispered to Greg,

"I have to sit on the aisle to take the offering."

Melinda slid in next to her mother. Greg sat next and Gerald took his job-reserved post on the aisle. The Mountainview choir entered from the back and walked up the aisle. They did not wear their gaudy purple and gold robes for the evening service.

Attendance on Sunday evenings was about half the size of Sunday morning. However, the number would have overwhelmed most Southern Baptist churches.

Chuck, Mountainview's animated choir director, walked in stage right and took his position next to Dothan's large pulpit. Chuck wore a sports jacket and open collar on Sunday evenings to visually express how progressive Mountainview was becoming. Dr. Dothan entered wearing a dark suit, crisp white shirt and presidential red tie. He balanced the progressive visual of Chuck. Dr. Dothan sat on a wooden chair that was as close to a kingly throne as existed in this part of Houston.

The choir sang, seated, stood, and sang some more. Brother Gerald and his fellow deacons took the offering before Dr. Dothan mounted his wooden chariot to engage the Enemy one more time.

There was no opening joke and three points tonight. Instead he led with,

"My talk tonight, like many of our tempers lately, will be short."

Old Lester Holt, who punctuated almost every sentence Dothan ever spoke, delivered his usual, "Amen!" and was slightly embarrassed by the laugh that followed.

"Thank you Lester, I needed that," Dothan acknowledged. "All of you are aware we are hosting the Southern Baptist Convention here in Houston in just a few weeks."

A few people clapped.

"Sure, you can applaud." Most of the congregation followed with applause.

"Well, one of my oldest friends, W.A. Criswell is being asked to consider serving as our next Convention president."

A few "in-the-know" mumbled.

"Many of you know the position on segregation he has taken since the 50's."

A smattering of spontaneous applause broke out.

"Well I forwarded a copy of a book to my friend which recently came into my possession. He called me yesterday to thank me and tell me something I wanted to share with you. He said, wait - I wrote this down so I would get it right, he said, 'I have enlarged my sympathies and my heart during the past few years.' I think that means he is changing his mind.

I invited someone to join us tonight. He is a former member of Mountainview that I, for one, would love to see return."

Surely he's not talking about me, Greg thought. But like Dr. Criswell, Greg had changed. Regardless of what was coming he was no longer afraid. The little boy who prayed not to be called on to pray had gone the way of his Roy Roger's Mineral City plastic men.

"You may have read about him in the paper or

seen his handiwork in our suddenly more sunny rear parking lot," Dothan said.

A couple of boos were heard.

"Sgt. Greg Henderson, United States Air Force, come up here and join me."

Gerald stepped into the aisle as Greg rose and stepped up on the platform next to Dothan. A couple of more low boos were heard and ignored by Dothan.

"Greg here, was wounded in Vietnam. He is a decorated medic who has saved lives and helped to bring many of our boys back home."

Greg looked down at Melinda who rolled her eyes to make him smile but she could not hide the fact that she was a very proud girlfriend.

Applause countered the former boos.

"But none of that is why I asked Greg to come up here. Many of our young men have served in Vietnam and many of you older men served in Korea and World War II. I said earlier that I sent Dr. Criswell a copy of a book and that he called to thank me. Well the book came from Greg. Would you share the story of the book with us Greg?"

Applause. Greg thanked Dr. Dothan and stepped into the borrowed old chariot. He did not waste time telling that this was as surprising an ambush as he experienced in the Delta or how humble this honoring made him feel.

Instead, he told them about his two Black friends. First about Chap and then about Emmett. Throughout his ten minute story, groups of two to eight people got up to leave at a time. Over eighty percent of the congregation stayed glued to his words.

Only the hardest hearts left in the room kept their eyes dry. When Greg finished, Dr. Dothan stood to applaud but was beat to his feet by Betsy, Gerald and Chuck. Chuck began to sing the Battle Hymn of the Republic. Within three notes the entire congregation, piano and organ joined. Greg walked down to be beside Melinda. Old Lester saluted Greg and "Amen"-ed.

> Glory, glory, hallelujah! Glory, glory, hallelujah!
> His truth is marching on.
>
> He has sounded forth the trumpet that shall never
> call retreat;
>
> He is sifting out the hearts of men before his
> judgment seat.
>
> Oh, be swift, my soul, to answer him; be jubilant
> my feet!
>
> Our God is marching on.

With the organ and piano continuing to play under, Dothan stepped to the microphone again to say, "Greg, you don't have to come back up here. You can see this from down there. Folks, this is Greg's friend's book."

Dothan held up a copy to another round of applause. "I am going to personally see to it that every messenger to the 1968 Southern Baptist Convention gets a copy of this book from Mountainview Baptist Church."

Everyone in the congregation, even the dry-eyed ones, thundered with applause. Chuck changed the singing.

> *There's a sweet, sweet Spirit in this place*
> *And I know that it's the Spirit of the Lord*
> *There are sweet expressions on each face*
> *And I know they feel the presence of the Lord*
>
> *Sweet Holy Spirit... sweet heavenly dove...*
> *Stay right here with us*
> *Filling us with Your love*
>
> *And for these blessings*
> *We lift our hearts in praise*
> *Without a doubt we know*
> *That we'll have been revived*
> *When we shall leave this place*

After the post-service handshakes and back slaps, Greg and Melinda reached her car in the parking lot. Gerald and Betsy pulled up alongside.

"I've got dinner all but ready at home. You kids come right over," Betsy said.

"We're going to Sonny Look's. I'm buying," Greg said.

"I'm not sure-" Gerald started.

"I'll get us there. Follow us," Greg said. Greg pulled out of the parking lot with Melinda on his good shoulder, Chap's book in the back seat, and Betsy's cooking far behind.

On the way they passed a police car who had pulled over a driver. The officer was Tommy and the ticketed motorist looked a lot like Joshua.

EPILOGUE

In the spring of 1983, Greg placed the 100,000[th] hard cover of "The Curse of Ham and Grits" by Rev. Chaplain (1st Lt.) Terrance L. "Chap" Bonner on the granite base under Chap's name on the wall of the Vietnam Veterans Memorial in Washington, D. C. Melinda was going to call over their two kids, Chap and Emily, to join them but she knew this was Greg's time to be with his second Black friend.

KEN BAILEY

POSTSCRIPT

This is a work of fiction. However, much of the tension and victories of this book were based on historical events. The summer of 1968 has been called "The Summer of Hate." Race riots, riots at the Republican Convention in Chicago and a second assassination. Shortly after midnight on June 6, presidential primary winner Senator Robert F. Kennedy was killed.

But earlier that day, the Southern Baptist Convention did meet in Houston, Texas and the messengers present approved the following statement by a vote of 5,687 to 2,119.

A Statement Concerning the Crisis in Our Nation

We recognize that no individual or organization can speak for all Baptists. The following represents the concern, confession, commitment, and appeal by the majority of the messengers meeting in Houston, Texas, June 5, 1968.

We Face a Crisis

Our nation is enveloped in a social and cultural revolution. We are shocked by the potential for anarchy in a land dedicated to democracy and freedom. There are ominous sounds of hate and violence among men and of unbelief and rebellion toward God. These compel Christians to face the social situation and to examine themselves under the judgment of God.

We are an affluent society, abounding in wealth and luxury. Yet far too many of our people suffer from poverty. Many are hurt by circumstance from which they find it most difficult to escape, injustice which they find most difficult to correct, or heartless exploitation which they find most difficult to resist. Many live in slum housing or ghettos of race or poverty or ignorance or bitterness that often generate both despair and defiance.

We are a nation that declares the sovereignty of law and the necessity of civil order. Yet we have had riots and have tolerated conditions that breed riots, spread violence, foster disrespect for the law, and undermine the democratic process.

We are a nation that declares the equality and rights of persons irrespective of race. Yet, as a nation, we have allowed cultural patterns to persist that have deprived millions of black Americans, and other racial groups as well, of equality of recognition and opportunity in the areas of education, employment, citizenship, housing, and worship. Worse still, as a nation, we have condoned prejudices that have damaged the personhood of blacks and whites alike. We have seen a climate of racism and reactionism develop resulting in hostility, injustice, suspicion, faction, strife, and alarming potential for bitterness, division, destruction, and death.

We Review Our Efforts

In the face of national shortcomings, we must nevertheless express appreciation for men of good will of all races and classes who have worked tirelessly and faithfully to create a Christian climate in our nation.

From the beginning of the Southern Baptist Convention, and indeed in organized Baptist life, we have affirmed God's love for all men of all continents and colors, of all regions and races. We have continued to proclaim that the death of Jesus on Calvary's cross is the instrument of God's miraculous redemption for every individual.

Inadequately but sincerely, we have sought in our nation and around the world both to proclaim the gospel to the lost and to minister to human need in Christ's name. Individually and collectively, we are trying to serve, but we have yet to use our full resources to proclaim the gospel whereby all things are made new in Christ.

We Voice Our Confession

"If my people, which are called by my name, shall humble themselves and pray, and seek my face, and turn from their wicked ways; then will I heal' 'from heaven, and will forgive their sin, and will heal their land" (2 Chron. 7:14).

The current crisis arouses the Christian conscience. Judgment begins at the house of God. Christians are inescapably involved in the life of the nation. Along with all other citizens we recognize our share of responsibility for creating in our land conditions in which justice, order, and righteousness can prevail. May God forgive us wherein we have failed him and our fellowman.

As Southern Baptists, representative of one of the largest bodies of Christians in our nation and claiming special ties of spiritual unity with the large conventions of

*Negro Baptists in our land, we have
come far short of our privilege in
Christian brotherhood.*

*Humbling ourselves
before God, we implore him to
create in us a right spirit of
repentance and to make us
instruments of his redemption,
his righteousness his peace, and
his love toward all men.*

We Declare Our Commitment

*The Christ we serve, the
opportunity we face, and the crisis we
confront, compel us to action. We
therefore declare our commitment,
believing this to be right in the sight of
God and our duty under the lordship
of Christ.*

*We will respect every
individual as a person possessing
inherent dignity and worth growing out
of his creation In the image of God.*

*We will strive to obtain and
secure for every person equality of
human and legal rights. We will
undertake to secure opportunities in
matters of citizenship, public services,
education, employment, and personal
habitation that every man may achieve
his highest potential as a person.*

We will accept and exercise

our civic responsibility as Christians to defend people against injustice. We will strive to insure for all persons the full opportunity for achievement according to the endowments given by God.

We will refuse to be a party to any movement that fosters racism or violence or mob action.

We will personally accept every Christian as a brother beloved in the Lord and welcome to the fellowship of faith and worship every person irrespective of race or class.

We will strive to become well informed about public issues, social ills, and divisive movements that are damaging to human relationships. We will strive to resist prejudice and to combat forces that breed distrust and hostility.

We will recognize our involvement with other Christians and with all others of goodwill in the obligation to work for righteousness in public life and justice for all persons. We will strive to promote Christian brotherhood as a witness to the gospel of Christ.

We Make An Appeal

Our nation is at the crossroads. We must decide whether

*we shall be united in goodwill,
freedom, and justice under God to
serve mankind or be destroyed by
covetousness, passion, hate, and
strife.*

*We urge all leaders and
supporters of minority groups to
encourage their followers to exercise
Christian concern and respect for the
person and property of others and to
manifest the responsible action
commensurate with individual dignity
and Christian citizenship.*

*We appeal to our fellow
Southern Baptists to join us in self-
examination under the Spirit of God
and to accept the present crisis as a
challenge from God to strive for
reconciliation by love.*

*We appeal to our fellow
Southern Baptists to engage in
Christian ventures in human
relationships, and to take courageous
actions for justice and peace.*

*We believe that a vigorous
Christian response to this national crisis
is imperative for an effective witness on
our part at home and abroad.*

*Words will not suffice. The time
has come for action. Our hope for
healing and renewal is in the*

*redemption of the whole of life. Let us
call men to faith in Christ. Let us dare to
accept the full demands of the love and
lordship of Christ in human
relationships and urgent ministry. Let us
be identified with Christ in the reproach
and suffering of the cross.*

*We therefore recommend to the
messengers of the Southern Baptist
Convention that:*

*1. We approve this statement
on the national crisis.*

*2. We rededicate ourselves to
the proclamation of the gospel, which
includes redemption of the individual
and his involvement in the social
issues of our day.*

*3. We request the Home
Mission Board to take the leadership in
working with the Convention agencies
concerned with the problems related to
this crisis in the most effective manner
possible and in keeping with their
program assignments.*

*4. We call upon individuals, the
churches, the associations, and the state
conventions to join the Southern Baptist
Convention in a renewal of Christian
effort to meet the national crisis.*

Twenty-seven years later the Baptists met again
and took the spirit of the 1968 resolution to its correct

conclusion.

Resolution On Racial Reconciliation

On The 150th Anniversary Of The Southern Baptist Convention

June 1995

WHEREAS, Since its founding in 1845, the Southern Baptist Convention has been an effective instrument of God in missions, evangelism, and social ministry; and

WHEREAS, The Scriptures teach that Eve is the mother of all living (Genesis 3:20), and that God shows no partiality, but in every nation whoever fears him and works righteousness is accepted by him (Acts 10:34-35), and that God has made from one blood every nation of men to dwell on the face of the earth (Acts 17:26); and

WHEREAS, Our relationship to African-Americans has been hindered from the beginning by the role that slavery played in the formation of the Southern Baptist Convention; and

WHEREAS, Many of our Southern Baptist forbearers defended the right to own slaves, and either participated in, supported, or acquiesced in the particularly inhumane nature of American slavery; and

WHEREAS, In later years Southern Baptists failed, in many cases, to support, and in some cases opposed, legitimate initiatives to secure the civil rights of African-Americans; and

WHEREAS, Racism has led to discrimination, oppression, injustice, and violence, both in the Civil War and throughout the history of our nation; and

WHEREAS, Racism has divided the body of Christ and Southern Baptists in particular, and separated us from our African-American brothers and sisters; and

WHEREAS, Many of our congregations have intentionally and/or unintentionally excluded African-Americans from worship, membership, and leadership; and

WHEREAS, Racism profoundly distorts our understanding of Christian morality, leading some Southern Baptists to believe that racial prejudice and discrimination are compatible with the Gospel; and

WHEREAS, Jesus performed the ministry of reconciliation to restore sinners to a right relationship with the Heavenly Father, and to establish right relations among all human beings, especially within the family of faith.

Therefore, be it RESOLVED, That we, the messengers to the Sesquicentennial meeting of the

Southern Baptist Convention, assembled in
Atlanta, Georgia, June 20-22, 1995, unwaveringly
denounce racism, in all its forms, as deplorable
sin; and

Be it further RESOLVED, That we affirm the
Bible's teaching that every human life is sacred,
and is of equal and immeasurable worth, made in
Gods image, regardless of race or ethnicity
(Genesis 1:27), and that, with respect to salvation
through Christ, there is neither Jew nor Greek,
there is neither slave nor free, there is neither male
nor female, for (we) are all one in Christ Jesus
(Galatians 3:28); and

Be it further RESOLVED, That we lament and
repudiate historic acts of evil such as slavery from
which we continue to reap a bitter harvest, and we
recognize that the racism which yet plagues our
culture today is inextricably tied to the past; and

Be it further RESOLVED, That we apologize to
all African-Americans for condoning and/or
perpetuating individual and systemic racism in our
lifetime; and we genuinely repent of racism of
which we have been guilty, whether consciously
(Psalm 19:13) or unconsciously (Leviticus 4:27);
and

Be it further RESOLVED, That we ask
forgiveness from our African-American brothers
and sisters, acknowledging that our own healing is
at stake; and

Be it further RESOLVED, That we hereby commit ourselves to eradicate racism in all its forms from Southern Baptist life and ministry; and

Be it further RESOLVED, That we commit ourselves to be doers of the Word (James 1:22) by pursuing racial reconciliation in all our relationships, especially with our brothers and sisters in Christ (1 John 2:6), to the end that our light would so shine before others, that they may see (our) good works and glorify (our) Father in heaven (Matthew 5:16); and Be it finally RESOLVED, That we pledge our commitment to the Great Commission task of making disciples of all people (Matthew 28:19), confessing that in the church God is calling together one people from every tribe and nation (Revelation 5:9), and proclaiming that the Gospel of our Lord Jesus Christ is the only certain and sufficient ground upon which redeemed persons will stand together in restored family union as joint-heirs with Christ (Romans 8:17).

After the passing of the resolution, Reverend Gary Frost offered a gracious acceptance.

Reverend GARY FROST: On behalf of my black brothers and sisters, we accept your apology and we extend to you our forgiveness in the name of our lord and savior, Jesus Christ. Ephesians Chapter 4, Verses 31 and 32, say let all bitterness and wrath and anger and clamor and evil speaking be put away from you with all malice, and be kind, one to another, tender-hearted, forgiving one another, even as God, for Christ's sake, hath forgiven you.

Because of Jesus Christ our Lord and Savior and his great love toward us, we extend that same love, forgiveness, grace and mercy towards you. We pray that the genuineness of your repentance will be reflected in your attitudes and in your actions. We forgive you, for Christ's sake, amen.

ABOUT THE AUTHOR

Ken Bailey

Author, Director, and Producer Ken Bailey began working in television while at Baylor University in 1966. His work as a producer includes PBS series, *Houston Remember When*, cable series *Easy Growing,* and projects for CBS, History Channel, and *48 Hours with Dan Rather.*

Son of Texas photographer Marvin Bailey (Bob and Marvin Bailey Collection - Briscoe Center for American History) gave him an early appreciation for visual story telling. This can be experienced in his films, like the award-winning *Tango Nights* and *The Deed* - the story of God's Mercy Store.

Ken Bailey is the founder of the Texas Christian Film Festival hosted by Houston's Bethany Christian Church.

In the late 1990's Ken made a commitment to focus on writing. His first musical "Christmas, Party of One" premiered to sold-out audiences during a six-week run in Houston and continues on to entertain and encourage across the country. His first novel, "I Flunked Sunday School", returned him to film where he served as executive producer on the movie version which won best feature film at Secret City Film Festival in Tennessee.

In non-fiction *Jesus…and the Word <u>was</u> God* was a special project he completed with his oldest granddaughter Emily.

This project was followed by *Dancing with Baptists* and Christmas novella based on his popular musical, now re-titled, *Manger in the Mall.* The story of two aging Baby Boomers who are outraged at the way Baby Jesus has been de-focused in favor of the fat guy in the red suit. Unfortunately their nativity booth complete with baby doll, "Picture Yourself with Jesus" is not the life-changing event they had hoped would happen.

Ken Bailey hopes all of his projects honor his Lord and Savior Jesus Christ and encourage, entertain, and offer hope, love and joy to readers everywhere.

ACKNOWLEDGMENTS

The author wishes to thank:

Melissa Larson

Patty Tuel Bailey

Jeannette Clift George

and Believer Artists everywhere

Ken Bailey:

www.KenBaileyBooks.com

www.Facebook.com/KenBailey1

www.YouTube.com/KenBaileyWriter